"How about a ride?
I'll take you home in style."

She pointed to the Hotel Danieli. "I'm practically on my front porch now."

"Oh, come on. We'll take the long way home."

Her first instinct was to disappear quickly, but she couldn't leave his side. "All right," she said.

As they descended the steps, Justin took her hand. The electricity of his touch left Lindy feeling almost dizzy. A tenor aria from a passing gondolier floated on the deepening shadows. Justin pulled her next to him as they waited quayside for a boat, putting his arm around her shoulder. Without thinking, Lindy leaned into him, tilting her face toward his.

For a moment, their eyes locked and Lindy felt sure she'd stopped breathing. As if powerless against a magnetic force, she drew closer to him. Closer...

Dear Reader,

Your enthusiastic reception of SECOND CHANCE AT LOVE has inspired all of us who work on this special romance line and we thank you.

Now there are *six* brand new, exciting SECOND CHANCE AT LOVE romances for you each month. We've doubled the number of love stories in our line because so many readers like you asked us to. So, you see, your opinions, your ideas, what you think, really count! Feel free to drop me a note to let me know your reactions to our stories.

Again, thanks for so warmly welcoming SECOND CHANCE AT LOVE and, please, *do* let me hear from *you*!

With every good wish,

Carolyn Nichols

Carolyn Nichols
SECOND CHANCE AT LOVE
The Berkley/Jove Publishing Group
200 Madison Avenue
New York, New York 10016

P.S. Because your opinions *are* so important to us, I urge you to fill out and return the questionnaire in the back of this book.

CRYSTAL FIRE
VALERIE NYE

SECOND CHANCE AT LOVE
BOOK

Second Chance at Love books are published by
The Berkley/Jove Publishing Group,
200 Madison Avenue, New York, NY 10016

· 1 ·

MELINDA THORNE, LINDY to her friends and family, settled into the deep red cushions of the motorboat-taxi as it plowed through the water. A small smile of enchantment touched her lips as her gaze arced slowly back and forth across the Grand Canal.

Venice at twilight shimmered in a translucent mauve. The sun's last rays danced on the water and cast lavender shadows on the unbroken row of Gothic and Byzantine buildings. It was hard to get used to, but this wide ribbon of water was the main thoroughfare of a bustling city. All sizes and speeds of boats passed, from lumbering water-buses to one-man skiffs. Magically, they avoided collision.

"Oh, isn't it wonderful!" she blurted, scarcely aware of her own voice, forgetting for a moment that she shared the *motoscafo*, the water-taxi, with her older sister and brother-in-law and their ten-year-old twins.

Beside her, Celine fussed at the fidgeting children,

1

ever the mother hen, Westchester or Venice. "Now, Tammy, Todd. I can't have you standing up like that." Celine had turned thirty in the spring, and she took it very seriously.

"Listen to your mother," Steven said absently. He was trying to communicate with the grinning pilot over the thrum of the engine. The man nodded and chuckled at the American's fractured Italian, winking when he caught Lindy's eye.

In spite of herself, she had to laugh. But her amusement swiftly died as the mustachioed man practically ignored the traffic to ogle her. His appreciative eye traveled from her white sandals up slim, tanned legs to the lines of her green linen dress. Disconcerted, she crossed her arms and pointedly looked away. What she definitely did not want on this trip was complications.

Lindy didn't realize how striking she appeared. At age twenty-six, she was beginning to fulfill her promise as a woman, breasts and hips curving firmly. Although she was small-boned and only of medium height, her bearing did not suggest fragility. Her blue green eyes, wide and round, seemed luminous in the fading light. The wind gently fluffed her cap of soft, dark honey curls.

"Get ready, everybody," Steven suddenly called. "In a minute you'll see the Rialto Bridge."

Glancing sideways at the pilot, Lindy was relieved to see that he had remembered his duty. Only now and then did he peek hopefully in her direction.

"It should be . . . there! There it is."

Almost eerily, the bridge materialized out of the shadows, an inverted V spanning the canal. At that moment, the lights came on and the arched colonnade sprang to life in a wash of pale gold. Lindy gasped in delight.

Leaning across Celine, Steven nudged his sister-in-law. "Now see?" he demanded triumphantly. "Aren't you glad you came?"

She smiled but didn't answer. It was her first taste of the city, and she didn't want to squander it by thinking about the reason she'd needed such a break in the first place. There'd be more than enough time for such thoughts later. She resolved to let the bewitching spell of Venice work on her now and revitalize her senses. She was pleased to realize that she'd made the right decision in accompanying her sister's family on Steven's business trip. The architectural knowledge of her brother-in-law, a city planner, certainly added to her enjoyment of Venice, and she'd quickly been infected by Steven's enthusiasm for the stunning buildings around them.

"Oh, look!" she suddenly exclaimed, amazed by the constant diversions Venice offered. She pointed to the facade of one house, its Gothic arches gloriously lit. Strings of tiny lights stretched around a floating café nearby, where people swayed and sang a sentimental tune. One young man waved to her, and she impulsively returned the gesture. He rose, as if to follow, but the boat was already moving away.

"You'll have to watch out for these guys," Steven warned, half serious. "Love 'em and leave 'em is their motto—they're notorious for it."

He surveyed the canal judiciously, having said more than he cared to in front of the children. "Around that bend...I think our hotel is just beyond. Three doors down from Saint Mark's Square."

Gradually the canal widened, spilling into a vast, dark bay. St. Mark's was a blur as they sped past, but Lindy got a glimpse of the stately basilica, with its towering campanile. The *motoscafo* stopped abruptly at a mooring before a deep-cinnamon-colored building. Bowing porters escorted them into the lobby of the Royal Danieli Excelsior, Lindy's sandals clicking softly on the buffed marble floor.

"*Per favore,*" Steven announced to the desk clerk, with no attempt to tame his atrocious accent. "Mr. and Mrs. Marsh and family, and Miss Thorne."

With more bowing, they were whisked to their rooms.

"Listen, everybody," Steven called, just as Lindy was about to close her door. "Are you hungry?"

"Starved."

"Yeah!"

"Sure am."

"Okay, okay. Tell you what: I have to call Signor Gilberti; he wanted to welcome us as soon as we got settled. How about if I ask him to suggest a little restaurant for our meeting?"

"Signor Gilberti, eh?" Celine asked playfully, glancing at her sister. "One of those suave Latin-lover types?"

Rolling her eyes, Lindy stifled a groan.

"No, no, dear," Steven chuckled. "He's a short little guy...looks something like the butcher we used to go to on Second Avenue in the City. I think his youngest son just left home last year."

"Oh...then he's married." Celine shot a quick, disappointed look at Lindy, who determined to ignore it.

"Very."

"Oh, well. Tell him we need half an hour to freshen up."

Once in her room, Lindy slipped out of her dress, then splashed water into the beige marble sink and dabbed at her face and arms. Flicking at her tousled hair with a brush and touching her lips lightly with color, she couldn't help notice the tingle of excitement inside her. What to wear? Something special for her first night in Venice...

Finally she chose a white eyelet sundress, narrow-strapped and smocked at the waist. It showed off her tan nicely, and it had a matching triangular shawl to pacify Celine.

When she was ready, a glance at the ceramic clock on the night table told her she had a few minutes to spare. The tall window beckoned, and she leaned out a tiny balcony, sniffing the sea-freshened air, staring at the twinkling lights.

It was hard to believe that yesterday she was in New York, and two days before that, home....

A melancholy frown flitted across her features. Home. Well, it *had* been home, the upstate village and the radio station. More than that, it had been her universe for a

long time. And how desperately she'd needed it, clung
to it, after her last world had exploded.

The memory of a face invaded her mind, and with it
his name, as blunt and mournful as a foghorn—Blair.
Quickly, she banished it. Oh no, you don't, she thought.
He wouldn't ruin this for her, too.

Suddenly, mercifully, Steven's polite knock anchored
her back into the present.

"Lindy?" he called. "All set?"

She grabbed her woven straw clutch and followed his
voice out to the hall. Celine scanned her critically and
beamed approval.

"You look lovely. The men will be falling all over
you."

"Please, Celine . . ."

"Come on, gang." Herding them all together, Steven
ushered his flock down to the lobby.

A short stroll down the quay brought them to St.
Mark's Square, and they walked quickly to its center.
People swarmed about them. Lindy stopped suddenly
and slowly turned in a circle, enthralled by what she
saw. Here, she sensed, was the heart of Venice. It beat
with the pulse of three different bands scattered around
its periphery. It rocked with the laughter of revelers on
holiday. In the play of light and shadow, she could see
an ever-changing mystery, now perfectly illuminated,
now shrouded in darkness.

"Aunt Lindy, come on. This way."

The tables in front of Florian's were crowded with
late diners. When Steven whispered to the head waiter,
an empty spot appeared, and Lindy slid gratefully into
the wicker-backed chair.

"Well, what'll we eat? Spaghetti? Lasagna?"

"Steven, really. It's after nine o'clock."

"That's the dinner hour in Italy, my dear. Perfectly
all right. So what'll it be, kids?"

"Pizza!"

Lindy was in the mood for something more adven-
turous, but she didn't want to tear her attention away

from the lively square long enough to make a decision. She glanced up only for a moment when Steven handed her a glass of red wine.

"Bardolino. Excellent in these parts, I hear. Well, let's drink to Venice and all her fascinations."

Lindy sipped. A perfect toast. Already she was captivated.

"Good evening, good evening!"

"Signor Gilberti!" Steven rose and pumped the hand of the rotund little man who stood before him. "Ladies, I'd like you to meet Signor Ugo Gilberti. Sir, this is my wife, Celine, and my sister-in-law, Miss Melinda Thorne."

The Italian inclined his head in a deep gesture. "It is one hundred percent my pleasure, *signora e signorina.*"

While Steven introduced the twins, Lindy studied Gilberti. There was an air of efficiency about him, and he held his round, balding head high with pride. A neatly clipped mustache curved bravely over his upper lip, defying the process that was removing the dark hair from his pate. At Steven's invitation, he sat directly opposite his American counterpart, at the other end of the table from Lindy and Celine. After a few perfunctory questions about their trip, he held out his hands, offering apologetically, "Business." He and Steven bent over the buff linen cloth, speaking in low, serious tones.

Lindy's gaze had already wandered back to the square, drawn to the energetic band conductor nearby. With sweeping waves of his baton he guided the small orchestra through "Santa Lucia." When the last sweet strains had died, he accepted the applause with nonchalant grace, certain it was no more than his due.

Leaning forward, Celine whispered, "Don't be too obvious about it, but look over your left shoulder. There's a guy really staring at you and he looks——"

"Celine." Lindy closed her hand over her sister's. "I love you dearly, but sometimes you are a royal pain in the you-know-what." She smiled to take away the sting of her words. "Look, hon. I came here for a change of scenery, to relax and see the sights. We've been here—what?—two hours, and already Venice is charming me. It's such an incredible place; I'm crazy about it. And to tell you the truth, the last thing I want is some man to distract me from all this beauty."

The piazza tugged at her again with its swirling activity, and she rested her chin on her palm, a bemused smile on her lips. All the others at the table were forgotten as she watched the people moving about.

A scraping of chairs on the stone pavement brought her back. Tilting her head, she saw the men rise to greet a tall stranger who approached their table. Signor Gilberti seemed a little flustered. His small eyes darted nervously back and forth, and he muttered something in Italian.

"Dear friends," he said at last, without enthusiasm, "permit me the honor to introduce Signor Justin DiPalma. Signor, Mr. Steven Marsh and..."

Gilberti's voice was lost in the vast square as Lindy found herself staring at DiPalma. He towered over the other men by a full eight inches. His hair was black and silky straight, just covering the top of his ears. His smooth olive skin stretched over high cheekbones. He moved easily but impatiently under a lightweight white turtleneck and a pearl gray jacket. Lindy didn't fail to notice that his dark brows and his mouth were set in annoyance, if not anger.

"...Signorina Melinda Thorne."

His nod of acknowledgment was no different for her than for the others, but Lindy thought she detected a flicker in his intent eyes. She swallowed hard, trying to manage a feeble *buona sera,* but the words wouldn't come, and she was reduced to a nod herself.

Gilberti reeled off a spate of irritated Italian, but DiPalma stopped him in midstream. "Please," he said, his mellow baritone edged with control, "let's not snub your guests. Speak in English."

Lindy started, realizing that he was an American. An extra chair was pulled to the table as the waiter brought their order. Welcoming the confusion, Lindy took a moment to catch her breath.

What in the world was coming over her? She'd been ignoring the amorous glances of good-looking men since she set foot in Venice. Why now, all of a sudden, was a casual, polite nod from a rather uninterested stranger affecting her like this? With surprise and faint embarrassment, she noticed that her heart was thudding and she felt flushed. She couldn't resist another glance at him. He was so obviously trying to hold his temper. He'd slipped off his jacket against the warm night air, and the muscles in his shoulders strained with the effort to keep himself in check. Through it all, he radiated a vitality that drew Lindy like a magnet.

She felt Celine's knowing smirk and looked up to confirm it.

"Lindy!" Celine whispered behind a cupped hand. "Isn't he gorgeous?"

Lindy frowned a warning and deliberately focused her attention on the dish before her. The Venetian-style pizza was thick-crusted, basted with tomato sauce, and topped with paper-thin slices of prosciutto and cheese. It looked and smelled delicious, but curiously, she wasn't hungry anymore. Instead, she concentrated on her wine and tried not to get caught staring at Justin DiPalma.

Gilberti was offended, and his accent became more pronounced.

"Signor, I have meet with my friends from America and we no ask you. You make *il disturbo*, signor. Not good for digestion."

DiPalma paid no attention to the shorter man's righteously flapping arms. He directed himself to Steven.

"Mr. Marsh, I must apologize to you for interrupting your dinner. And to you too, Mrs. Marsh, Miss Thorne—" Was it her imagination, or did he pause a moment as if to photograph her with his eyes? "—and I promise to make it up to you. All I ask, Mr. Marsh, is that you give me equal time to state my case. Signor Gilberti is an honorable man, sincere in his wish to make Venice a better place." He stopped and inhaled a deep breath. It seemed to calm him, and when he spoke again his voice was warmer. "I have the same intentions, but different methods. At least hear my side before you go ahead with any plans."

Rising, DiPalma scooped up his jacket. A smile ruffled his mouth. "You're staying at the Danieli, aren't you? They have a lovely rooftop dining terrace. Would you have lunch with me there tomorrow? All of you . . ."

This time Lindy was sure: his emphasis on *all* was addressed to her. And she couldn't deny the spark of excitement at the prospect of seeing him again. As he turned and threaded his way through the crowd, she watched his broad back until he disappeared into the throng.

"Many pardons," Gilberti moaned, wringing his plump hands. "That one, he is—how do you say?—a maker of trouble. He gives me grief, *ogni volta*, each time I see him. Please excuse . . ."

Lindy bit her lip to stifle a grin, and then she straightened, startled by the thought that flashed through her mind. The only grief that man could give her was not showing up tomorrow at lunch. Venice with its endless charms had faded into the background when Justin DiPalma walked onto the scene.

- 2 -

SHADING HER EYES from the diamond-bright sun, Lindy gazed out over the city. The rooftop view gave her a different perspective of Venice. From this vantage point, she wasn't aware of the canals that wove between the buildings. She saw only the domes and spires of churches, silver and gold against the peacock blue sky, and coral-tiled roofs slanting into slate gray ones.

She swiveled to scan the expanse of the lagoon. In the distance, the island chain—the *lidi*—guarded the Queen of the Adriatic as faithfully as it had for centuries.

"Lindy, come sit. We're having an aperitif."

"In a minute, Celine."

"I thought you wanted to get here early, to have a drink before our handsome host——"

"I'm coming."

In truth, Lindy felt edgy and anxious, and she was thoroughly disgusted with herself for it. She had been looking forward to a rest of mind, soul, and body, and here she was feeling fizzy inside. All because of a man who had simply invited her to lunch—along with two other people!

"Ridiculous," she muttered to herself.

Pasting on a nonchalant smile, she joined Celine and Steven at the table.

"Campari and soda, *per favore,*" she said to the attending waiter.

"That's more like it," her sister nodded complacently. "Signor DiPalma ought to be here any moment now. Don't fuss with your hair. You look fine. You know, one advantage of a late lunch is that you have the entire place almost to yourself. Personally, I like the idea of a siesta. This is the first nap the twins have taken in *years,* but it's probably jet lag. . . ."

From long-standing practice, Lindy tuned out Celine's chatter. When the Campari was placed before her, she took a long sip. It had been an exhausting morning. She'd thought she had smoothed the kinks of the journey last evening after a warm bath and a solid sleep, but flexing her leg muscles, she grimly reminded herself that it wasn't quite so.

After breakfast, while Steven met with Ugo Gilberti, they'd gone on a self-styled tour of St. Mark's Basilica and the Doges' Palace. Going up one steep staircase, then down another, they covered what seemed like miles of corridors under vaulted ceilings covered with mosaics and gilt. The experience was beautiful and awesome, engaging her total attention. For three hours, Justin DiPalma had barely entered her mind.

Then, as Celine supervised the children's meal and settled them down for the petite Italian babysitter, Lindy started getting ready for lunch. She chose a strapless aquamarine shift. Worrying that it was too "uncovered," she threw on a matching short-sleeved jacket, then defiantly yanked it off. She added extra tint to her cheeks and lips, ignoring the mocking voice inside that wondered why. She brushed her honey-colored hair three different ways, then frowned in exasperation and combed it hurriedly with her fingers.

Now she sat waiting on the nearly deserted dining terrace of the Danieli. Her fingers drummed distractedly on her crossed knee, half in anticipation, half in dread.

"Steven was really intrigued—weren't you, dear?" Celine was saying, patting her husband's hand. "I mean, when the company sent him here, he had no idea there would be any conflict." Her laugh was close to a giggle. "Isn't it exciting?"

"You know, Celine, that Gilberti thinks this DiPalma is an out-and-out reactionary. Ruthless and dangerous."

"I don't believe it."

As the other two looked up in surprise, Lindy fumbled to qualify her flat statement. "That is, what I meant was, he just seemed too concerned and . . . and polite to be ruthless or dangerous."

Steven shrugged. "Maybe. At any rate we'll soon find out. Here he comes now."

With long, purposeful strides, Justin DiPalma was approaching their table. He wore a superbly tailored cream-colored suit and a small, welcoming smile. Lindy took a deep breath and tried to relax. It worked on her outer self, but not on the inner.

"Mr. Marsh. How good of you to accept my invitation," he said in a low, composed voice. The two men gripped hands, and DiPalma turned to Celine.

"Mrs. Marsh," he murmured, lightly taking her hand. "I'm glad you could join us."

Celine twittered appreciatively, but he was already bending over Lindy. His fingers were cool and smooth as they touched hers. She smiled tentatively, and he rewarded her with a larger smile of his own. His teeth, even and white, contrasted pleasingly with his olive skin. His enigmatic gaze stayed on her for an extra beat as he took the chair to her right.

"If you haven't ordered yet, I suggest the broiled shrimp. It's a specialty here. Giancarlo!" he called, raising his arm. "A Soave di Verona, I think. And we'll order now."

Something in his manner soothed Lindy. He seemed so confident, not the least bit hesitant. He took charge with quiet assurance, without overpowering them.

"Now tell me," he said, unbuttoning his jacket and settling comfortably in his chair. "What sights did you see today?"

"Well, we went all through Saint Mark's," Celine began, happily enumerating on her fingers. "And the clock tower and the palace, and let me tell you, we don't have anything like that..."

While her sister spoke, Lindy found DiPalma's gaze returning to her again and again, as if he were trying to draw a response from her. In her mind, it only accentuated the annoyance she felt with herself.

Good God! she fumed inwardly. Here she'd spent nearly the whole two previous years on the radio, talking to everybody from missionaries to murderers, but in this man's presence all she could do was sit completely tongue-tied.

But there was a difference, she reluctantly admitted. The talk show had been business; this was purely personal. And when was the last time she'd conversed with a man without the protective gulch of business stretching between them?

There was only one thing to do, she decided. She'd simply have to think in terms of interviewing him.

The *gamberoni arosti* had arrived, large stuffed shrimp in an herbed sauce. When it had been tasted and exclaimed over, Lindy took a sip of wine and smiled pleasantly at DiPalma.

"You sound like an American and look like an Italian. Tell me, which are you?"

"Actually, both," he replied, laughing. "I have dual citizenship: Italian from my father and American from my mother. I grew up in San Francisco, went to school in California."

"Ah, that explains it. So how did you happen to come to Venice?"

"I've lived in Rome ever since I got my degree in architecture about nine years ago. I work for a consortium called *Bell'Italia*. We're concerned with the preservation of all those wonderful ancient buildings—like the ones you saw this morning."

"Concerned? How do you mean?"

DiPalma drank some of his wine and tilted his glass toward the domes of St. Mark's.

"The twentieth century is hard on old stone—pollution, expanding population, the ravages of time itself . . ." For a moment, his expression sobered and he became preoccupied with the basilica. Then, his mouth twitching with amusement, he lifted an eyebrow at Lindy, silently asking if she had any more questions.

A flush spread over her throat. So, on top of his self-possession he was also astute. She should have been furious with him, stringing her along, answering her probes, then letting her know he saw what she was doing. Narrowing her eyes, she studied him for a few seconds. His smile was without malice, almost apologetic.

Despite herself, Lindy responded, and not in anger. For the first time that afternoon, she felt at ease. She had the vague notion that a test had been passed, but she wasn't sure by whom—Justin DiPalma or Lindy Thorne.

"You know," Steven cut in, waving his fork, "Gilberti thinks you're a total scoundrel."

"Ah, yes, Signor Gilberti," Justin grimaced in good humor. "If he had his way, I'd be dangling from the top of the campanile, like the rogues of four centuries ago."

"For heaven's sake, why?" Celine gasped.

He shook his dark head. "The groups we represent don't see eye to eye, and that's putting it in the mildest terms possible." Focusing on Steven, he addressed him earnestly. "That's why I barged in so rudely last night. I had to have a chance to talk to you, Mr. Marsh. I know you're here as a consultant to Gilberti's organization, and believe me, I've done my homework. I've seen some of the recommendations you drew up for that cluster of towns in Ohio and that land development in Arizona. You know your stuff. You could probably bring just about any city into the modern age."

Steven shifted in his chair and cleared his throat, pretending not to be affected, but Lindy could see that he was flattered.

"Please, Mr. Marsh..." DiPalma paused, and when he continued his voice was quiet and firm. "Think twice before you work your modernization on *La Serenissima*. She is more than just a city, you know. By removing her from the centuries of her glory, you could be destroying her."

Blinking, Lindy regarded him with a speculative gaze. He was leaning slightly forward; his body seemed taut, straining to convince Steven. And in the brilliant afternoon light that seeped under the dining canopy, she could see his eyes clearly. They were not fiercely dark, as she had imagined the night before, but shades of amber and green. She wondered if their changing colors reflected his moods—and if they would glow as passionately for a woman as they did for Venice.

The thought startled her, and she plucked at the stem of her glass distractedly. What made her even think of such a thing? It wasn't like her at all. But then, she'd felt different ever since the sweeping ride down the Grand Canal last evening.

Lindy took a gulp of wine, her brows wrinkling. It was vacation euphoria, that's all. Having left her troubles along with her winter clothes in a trunk in Celine's attic, she was free to relax and enjoy life for the first time in years. That's why she'd felt almost intoxicated with the sights and smells and sounds of this remarkable city.

She should be grateful, she told herself. And yet...She barely recognized the woman who reacted so instinctively to Venice...and to Justin.

Already in her mind he had ceased to be merely Signor DiPalma. That alone set alarm bells ringing.

She quickly chastized herself. How could she possibly

let this happen? Just when she was beginning to get over Blair. Just when she'd proven to herself that her mother was wrong, that she COULD exist without a man to depend on.

No. It was better to nip it now, before it developed any further. No complications was the deal she'd made with herself. Draining her glass, she set it down decisively on the table.

"Lindy?"

She looked up, disoriented, as Celine called her name.

"Hon, Signor DiPalma asked you a question."

"Oh," she stammered. "I'm sorry." Recovering, she faced him with what she hoped was a noncommittal smile. "I guess the view hypnotized me. What did you say?"

Justin's keen appraisal unnerved her, and she fought to maintain her gaze. Finally, he softened and said mildly, "I asked what sights were on your itinerary for this afternoon."

"Oh," Lindy was relieved to be on neutral ground. "I don't know. What do you suggest?"

His arms spread expansively. "Ah, there is so much! But no one should come to *Venezia* without seeing how her sons painted her. Titian, Tintoretto, Carpaccio . . . Here, let me make you a list of churches and galleries."

Taking a slim notebook from his breast pocket, he tore out a piece of paper and began writing swiftly with a Florentine gold pen.

"You have a motorboat at your disposal, no? Just give this to the pilot."

Lindy glanced at the words, *Accademia, San Rocco, Santa Maria Gloriosa,* written in a bold and impatient script.

"Thank you."

"Yes, that's very kind of you," Celine added warmly. "And we've enjoyed our lunch so much."

"Oh, must you go now?"

Steven was already standing, offering his host a hand. "Afraid so . . . another meeting this afternoon." As

Justin opened his mouth to speak, Steven raised his palms. "Now, all I can promise you, signor, is that I will keep in mind what you've said today. I do want to hear all sides of the question. Will you be at the *Patria Grande* reception day after tomorrow?"

Justin frowned for a moment, then a grin overtook his features. "Is that an invitation, Mr. Marsh?"

"Why . . . why, I suppose it is. Certainly. Why not? We can use all sorts of input. After all, it's only fair, right?"

For some reason, Lindy was glad her brother-in-law hadn't brushed him off. She abandoned the thought before she had time to analyze it.

They all stood now, offering and accepting thanks. Celine took her husband's arm and started across the deserted terrace, leaving Justin to escort her sister.

His fingers lightly pressed on Lindy's elbow as he guided her to the exit. Yards short, he abruptly stopped, turning her to face him.

"Listen, that list I gave you is a good start," he began, still holding her arm, "but to really see Venice, you have to explore the small canals and alleyways, the shops below the Rialto—places where the Venetians and not just the tourists go. What do you think?"

Lindy was poised for a polite refusal, but the words never left her lips. His gentle fingers on her arm, his soft voice urging her, his eyes serenely compelling, Lindy's defenses began to shred.

Justin smiled easily.

"I'm feeling optimistic today, so I'll assume you really want to say Yes. How's tomorrow sound? I'm taking the day off. I'll pick you up here, at the hotel, at eleven."

Before Lindy could protest—or even decide if she wanted to—he led her to Celine and Steven.

"*Arrivederci, signorina,*" he murmured, lightly touching his lips to her hand. "Until tomorrow."

He spun and was gone. Celine stared at her sister, saucer eyed.

"Did he say— Are you——"

"Oh, hush, Celine," Lindy answered crossly. But the same questions hammered at her too. Was she going with him?

All she could think of was his cool lips on her fingers. How could they have left such a burning imprint on her?

- 3 -

LINDY EMERGED FROM her bath and wrapped herself in a thick terry robe. Padding across her room, she flopped onto the chaise longue with a grateful sigh.

"Mmm, relief." She ran her fingers over the pale aqua silk of the chaise and wriggled her liberated toes.

The afternoon had skidded by. The tour of the art galleries and churches had produced a sort of time warp. She'd gazed in admiration at Renaissance paintings of Venice, then stepped outside to see those same scenes virtually unchanged in five centuries, viewing barges and gondolas ply the waters amidst the churches and palaces glowing in the peculiar apricot light that only native Venetian artists seemed to capture.

The hometown fellows painted her best, she decided. Justin was right.

Once his name sprang to the front of her mind, she realized that it had been lingering around the edges ever since lunch. Now that she was beyond Celine's radar, she felt a little freer to think about him. *Was* she going out with him tomorrow? It certainly hadn't been in her plans. But then again, one afternoon date did not signal the start of a grand complication or, for that matter, any relationship at all. Couldn't they be just two Americans exploring the quainter parts of the city?

"Why not?" Lindy murmured to herself. In this past year she'd proven adept in handling herself, in establishing boundaries. This Italian-American architect should be no problem. There was no reason not to go out with him just once. For fun. For companionship.

But if you only want companionship, a small voice inside her pointed out, you could go with your sister.

Lindy let her gaze drift out the window to the sparkling lagoon beyond. She found it vaguely disturbing that she couldn't get him out of her head, even when she tried . . . as if she were helpless, susceptible to his all-pervading presence.

But I'm *not* helpless, she reminded herself stubbornly. Not like before. Not as she had been with Blair.

That was it, wasn't it? A frown clouded her clear features. Blair had successfully disarmed and then crippled her with his charm, his facile reasoning, his total belief that he was always right. She'd felt susceptible from the day they'd met—a day, in fact, very much like this one.

Of course, the air at Lake George was cooler as it came whispering down from the emerald Adirondacks. And the light was translucent and not at all deceptive. But the sun shimmered just as brightly on the quiet water.

Lindy remembered shading her eyes against it, sitting in the cockpit of her small sailboat. She wore white shorts and scuffed Top-Siders and a Camp Wakenda T-shirt. It was her afternoon off from her job: teaching sailing at a summer camp near her Bolton Landing home. The wind was perfect, and she'd looked forward to a glide across the lake, just for fun, just for her. It was at the same time relaxing and invigorating. Lindy absorbed the healing sun, so pure she could smell and taste it.

A buzzing caught her attention, and she ran her expert gaze over the horizon. A large speedboat was bearing down, still comfortably far away but headed straight at her.

"He knows I have the right-of-way, doesn't he?" she muttered to herself as the crimson-hulled vessel neared. "Doesn't he?"

She remembered that she could even see the young man at the helm, his sun-bleached hair blowing in the wind, his bare, tanned chest partially concealed by the redheaded girl who was draped across his body. They were deep in a passionate embrace, totally oblivious to Lindy and her craft.

"Hey!" she screamed. "Hey!"

At the last moment, the speedboat veered, its powerful engine throbbing. The turbulence swamped the fragile sailboat, and Lindy was flung into the icy water. She surfaced, gasping from the cold. The motorboat was circling back toward her, slower now.

"You dumb jerk!" she yelled feebly. The lightweight sailboat was easily righted, and she climbed aboard, still shivering.

"Are you okay?" the young skipper called.

"Yes, no thanks to you."

He grinned, his arm still clamped to his companion's shoulder. His eyes were concealed by mirrored sunglasses. The redhead wore a vacuous stare and not much more.

"I suggest," he drawled, "that you learn more about sailing before you go out in the demon wind." With a jaunty wave, he revved the engine and was gone in a streak of scarlet.

"Wh—why you—"

Lindy felt no chill then, overcome by a steamy anger. She was no amateur. She'd been sailing for two-thirds of her twenty years. Besides, what did he know, a joy-riding preppie, out to impress his girl in his daddy's speedboat? Didn't he even realize that sailboats always have the right-of-way? No, he was more interested in the progress he was making with that girl.

To her great surprise, he showed up a few days later bearing what looked like a bushel of sweetheart roses. Lindy was nearly speechless. With sunglasses removed, his gray eyes revealed him to be older than she'd thought. Old enough to know better.

"You could have killed me the other day!"

With a smile that was just barely apologetic, he moved toward her.

"That auburn-haired witch had me under a spell. But the moment I laid eyes on you, I sent her packing. By the way, my name's Blair Talbot."

"How do you do? Don't you know about the right-of-way rule? And how did you find me, anyway?"

"Your T-shirt." His grin widened, and Lindy suddenly remembered the clammy tightness of her clothes after she'd been dumped in the lake. She flushed under her tan.

"It told me where to find you," he continued, proffering the roses. "So here I am. Will you accept this token of my very deep apology?"

He bowed theatrically, but when he looked up for her answer, Lindy detected a flash of sincerity. Not much, but enough to intrigue her.

"All right. But don't go speeding around the lake under the influence anymore, okay?"

Blair took her hand as if to shake it, but simply held it lightly. "It's a deal . . . with one string attached: You come to the Fourth of July dance at the club with me. We can discuss . . . rules."

It was a subject that would recur time after time in their relationship. To Blair, rules were pretty but useless figurines, and he was just the bull to go carousing through the china shop. He was blithely indifferent to the tenets that fell in his wake and thoroughly democratic in the selection of people he offended. He seemed to get the most satisfaction from defying family precepts that had held for generations—especially where suitable young women were concerned.

"Well, they've narrowed the marriage sweepstakes to a field of three: one from Vassar, one from Southampton, and one—they must be really reaching—from Virginia. They all bore me to death. You're the only person I have any fun with, Melinda!"

She had to admit they did have fun. Blair was superb at whatever he chose to do, and kicking up his heels was what he chose most often. The summer passed in a whirl of parties at the club and catered picnics and romantic midnight cruises on chartered boats. There was nothing simple about Blair's pleasures.

As Labor Day approached, he grew more and more restless. Lindy made no mention of his change in moods. Finally, it was he who broached the subject.

"If you want to know the truth, Melinda, this may be my last season of freedom. Father's pulled a dirty trick on me. He's been talking all summer about a Grand Tour, and just when I'm starting to pack for Europe, he informs me that what he has in mind is a tour of the companies his corporation owns. If this is Tuesday, it must be Talbot Mining." He stretched his long legs and sighed. "I think the man actually expects me to work for a living."

"The monster," Lindy said dryly.

"Isn't he though? But seriously, my dear, I *am* going to miss you."

With a start, Lindy realized she'd miss him too. He brought lightness to a heart that had been so often heavy. After her father's death six years earlier, her mother had shrunken into her shell, Celine had married and borne children, and Lindy had struggled more or less on her own to eventually get to college. It had not been an easy life.

But with Blair, every day was carefree. He spent money the way most people breathed: almost unconsciously, as if it were the most natural thing in the world and would never exhaust his supply. To a girl who skipped lunches to buy a new blouse, Blair was a heady experience.

He asked her to marry him on a moonlit August night, whispery with distant crickets. He had been kissing her for what seemed hours, and she was weak-kneed with longing for him. It was a totally new feeling, and all she could think was, if this was love, she wanted it to last forever.

They were married in late September on a golden afternoon. Her family was ecstatic, his aghast. Blair thoroughly enjoyed each and every reaction. They left for a Caribbean honeymoon, an endless, carefree summer, foolishly believing that the winter of reckoning could be postponed indefinitely. . . .

A polite jangling startled Lindy from her reverie. She blinked and focused her gaze. Twilight pressed lightly on the Venetian lagoon outside her hotel window. She reached for the ornate telephone.

"Hello?"

"Lindy, the twins are raring to go again. They claim they're starving—can you imagine? After all that pastry and those ices they gobbled down this afternoon! Anyway, Steven has a dinner meeting, so I thought we'd try out the hotel dining room. What do you say, would you like to join us?"

"Oh . . . dinner. Well . . . sure, Celine. That would be nice."

"Hey, are you all right? You sound a little vague."

Lindy sighed. The CIA is dying for talent, and she wastes it on me, she thought, unable to suppress a smile.

"Melinda?"

"I'm fine. I must have dozed a little, and I'm still drowsy."

"Oh. Meet you in the lobby at nine? Good, see you then."

Lindy switched on the dressing-table lamp and began brushing her hair. Despite her sister's quirks, she really did enjoy her company.

Dropping the hairbrush onto the table with a clatter, she stared at her reflection in the gilded mirror. Why was she so intent on denying it? She also enjoyed Justin's company. There! She'd admitted it frankly. Was it such a terrible thing? Did having fun with someone necessarily lead to pain and destruction?

"That's crazy," she told the woman in the mirror.

She'd shouldered her share of the blame for the fiasco her marriage to Blair had become. Her heart had been wide open, and she'd allowed him to come galloping in, toppling one absolute after another. She'd cleaned up the havoc alone. And she had a much stronger guard up now.

Sitting up straighter, she stroked moisturizer lightly over her skin. There was no reason on earth why she couldn't go out with Justin DiPalma tomorrow. He could show her parts of Venice she'd never discover on her own, and maybe even help her understand this beautiful enigma of a city. And if he happened to overstep the bounds she decided on, well, her communication skills were much improved from what they were two years ago. She would simply let him know she was interested only in friendship.

Only after her decision was made did Lindy identify the tingle in the pit of her stomach. It was anticipation.

- 4 -

LINDY GLANCED YET again at the porcelain clock on the dressing table, then checked it against her wristwatch. Ten fifty-five. The soft, taunting ticks told her both time-pieces were working, even though the last thirty minutes had seemed like eons.

"I started getting ready too soon," she muttered, glaring at her reflection in the mirror for the hundredth time. Suddenly the camisole-topped sundress she wore looked all wrong, the blush-pink gauze much too revealing for a casual date with an almost total stranger. Her gaze raked frantically over her wardrobe as her fingers pulled at the pearly buttons.

The telephone interrupted her halfway out of her dress. She froze a moment, then cleared her throat before answering.

"Yes?...Oh yes, thank you. Please tell the *signor* that I'll be right there."

Cradling the receiver, Lindy drew a deep breath. No time to change now. She refastened her dress.

"Ready or not, here I come."

She spotted him first. His hands resting on his hips, he stood in the lobby admiring the arches and scrolls of the ceiling. Lindy hesitated a moment as she stepped off the elevator, watching him in profile. Even standing still, Justin projected an energy and power that undeniably attracted her. As if he sensed her presence, he turned, easing into a smile as he walked toward her.

"Buon giorno, signorina." He took her hand in his briefly. "It's a lovely day, and you make it more so."

Unsure how to answer his gentle compliment, Lindy inclined her head in a small gesture of thanks. For all his unaccented English, his phrasing and mannerisms had a continental flavor, a romantic formality more reminiscent of the Old World than the New. She was not used to his style, but already she appreciated it. It gave her breathing room.

"I thought we might visit the shops near the Rialto Bridge, then have lunch at a special place I know. How would that be?"

"Fine," Lindy said, wishing she didn't sound so nervous. "That would be just fine."

They set off on foot, passing by the Doges' Palace along the wide waterfront court. Lindy was acutely aware of the strolling, chattering sightseers, the first tantalizing whiffs of lunch from the cafés, the brittle sunlight—and of Justin's lithe body moving beside her, first too quickly, then adjusting his pace to hers. She slipped on her sunglasses for whatever measure of protection they could give her.

Stealing a glance at his face, she noted his barely concealed pleasure as he lifted his gaze to the pink-and-white palace. It was the look of a man once again meeting an old, dear friend.

She was startled by a beating of wings, and as she stumbled, he caught her elbow to steady her.

"Wh—what?..."

Justin pointed. "There."

A flock of pigeons swept skyward, then spiraled down

toward the next group of willing tourists, the next scattered handful of corn.

Lindy laughed weakly. "It's almost as though they
have radar."

"Yes," he nodded, amused. "Actually, they need it
to tell friend from foe, the tourists who want to feed them
from the preservationists who want to do them in."

"The poor things. And which group do you belong
to?"

"I'm afraid that in my profession I am usually foe.
But today I am not DiPalma the architect, dedicated to
business, I'm just another tourist. And a long time it has
been...." He gave himself a moment to soak in the
surroundings. "Well, the pigeons are in luck. Today I
will forget my usual urges and consider myself neutral."

"That's comforting. For the pigeons, anyway."

They looked at each other and smiled in earnest. Lindy
loosened her iron-tight grasp on her handbag. She'd been
even more tense than she'd thought, and it was a relief
to relax a bit. But not much, because Justin still held her
arm.

"Here's our transportation."

He indicated a sleek black power skiff. A wiry, mustachioed man balanced easily in the cockpit, waiting.
Justin stepped into the boat, reaching a hand up to Lindy
on the dock. Her fingers clasped his, fitting the unknown
contours of his palm.

"This old monkey is Giacomo, our captain for the
day."

He translated his introduction for the old man, whose
face split in a wide grin. Lindy listened to Justin's lilting
Italian, nodding slightly when she heard "Signorina
Thorne." At his invitation she positioned herself on the
rear leather seat, and Justin sat beside her, his thigh
barely touching hers. She studiously looked toward the
basin, glad when the engine roared to life and drowned
out the thudding of her heart.

They traveled swiftly up the Grand Canal. The noise
made conversation impossible, for which Lindy was

deeply grateful. Justin pointed out various buildings with improvised sign language and quick shouts in her ear.

"Palazzo Grassi."

"What?"

"I said, Palazzo Grassi!"

The boat rocked in the choppy water just as he bent closer. His mouth grazed her earlobe. Startled, they both pulled away, almost apologetically.

This was positively ridiculous, Lindy thought. Why did she go into a state of shock every time this man touched her?

She felt relieved when the *motoscafo* slowed alongside the quay above the Ponte di Rialto. This time when he helped her out of the craft, she concentrated on the stone beneath her and not on the solid strength of his arm.

"This way."

He guided her past the base of the Rialto Bridge onto the avenue that lay beyond. Lindy caught her breath in delight. Here, just out of sight of the Grand Canal, stretched a street lined with shops. Striped awnings dipped protectively over the storefronts, sheltering sidewalk displays of vegetables and cheeses, pasta and flowers. It was swarming with life and Lindy delighted in the Venetian housewives, their string bags bulging with eggplants and tomatoes; the prim maids examining, selecting, giving crisp orders for delivery; and the aproned shopkeepers shouting the praises of their goods.

"Do you like it?" Justin asked, and Lindy noticed an almost hopeful glint in his green eyes.

"Oh, yes! It's wonderful."

They wandered among the milling crowd, sidestepping scampering children and their harried mothers. As they strolled by a coffee grinder, Lindy closed her eyes and sniffed with pleasure.

"You know, I could walk down this street and without watching tell you every store we passed, just by the wonderful smells."

"Ah," Justin pointed out, "but how much you would miss! Look there."

A round, dark-haired woman was impassively choosing flowers for a bouquet, carnations and daisies and shiny lemon leaves. The florist stood before her, wringing his hands and moaning, holding up first five fingers, then four, and finally three. The woman grinned, then the shopkeeper rolled his eyes and petitioned heaven, while she shoved money into his hand. Both finished the exchange with smiles of triumph on their faces.

"Oh, I wish I spoke Italian," Lindy laughed.

"Bargaining here is a real art form. This is one of the last places in Venice where it's accepted, unfortunately." Justin measured her for a moment, and his mouth curved slightly. "Would you like to try it?"

She bit her lip, tempted.

"I'd like to ... but do they understand English?"

"Probably, but it's better to do it in Italian. You only need a few words and ten fingers. Here, let me show you."

He scanned the flower stall and nodded toward the fat bunches of violets.

"See there? The sign says—what?—fifteen hundred lire? That's about a dollar twenty-five, way overpriced. What you do is offer him about a fourth of that. He'll come down, you'll go up, and if you get them for half-price, both of you will be happy. You see?"

"Well, I think so. . . . But what about the numbers? I don't know them in Italian."

"Do just what he does; use your hands. Listen, why don't I go first and you watch."

Giving her a conspiratorial wink, he strode confidently up to the display. The florist, a cigarette dangling from his lip, greeted him cordially. Justin chose a bunch of violets, then frowned and shook his head sadly. Looking wounded, the other man began his sales pitch. Justin raised his hand, five fingers spread.

Lindy was drawn away from the action in the flower stall to stare at Justin's hands. Beautiful, long-fingered and strong, they were capable and honest.

"Signorina?"

He was offering her the violets. She took them with a smile and brushed their velvety softness against her cheek.

"Grazie."

"Ah! You see? You do know some Italian."

"Only the basics."

"That's all you need—that and a few choice invectives." He thought a second and smiled. "Like this: *Che furto!* In the style of grand opera, you see? *Che furto!* Such robbery!"

"Che furto!" she repeated.

"Bene! Now try this: *Oltraggioso."*

"Ol—logio——"

"Oltraggioso. Outrageous. Here, watch my mouth: *Ol-tra-GIO-so."*

She stared at his lips, rounding in the shape of the word. So soft, almost a caress. Unconsciously, her lips conformed in the same curved lines. Slowly, nearly in silence.

Suddenly Lindy looked up. His eyes were directed at her mouth too, and he seemed nearly hypnotized. Something flared through his entrancement, something intense and potent. Only for a moment. Then he blinked, and it was gone.

"Well...yes." He cleared his throat. *"Oltraggioso.* I think you have it. Would you like to try it out on that greengrocer?"

She felt a little shaky, and she knew the burly greengrocer had nothing to do with it. Swallowing hard, she tried to laugh, to restore their former light mood.

"Grand opera, right?"

With more nonchalance than she felt, Lindy sauntered through the fruit stall, while Justin stood outside, arms crossed, watching her. She trailed her hand along a melon, pinched one of the plump black grapes, and hefted a large yellow peach in her palm.

"Quanto?" she idly asked the proprietor. "How much?"

He jerked his thumb at the sign: 600 lire.

"Che furto!" Lindy gasped. She held up one finger.

"Uno!" the grocer slapped his forehead in disbelief. He signaled five.

"Oltraggioso." Her eyebrows lifted in disdain. Two fingers.

The grocer lowered his voice and spread his arms, a reasonable man. He cajoled, he smiled winningly, and all the while, Lindy calmly shook her head.

"No, *signor,*" she said, a reasonable person herself. Three fingers. *"Finito."*

Sighing and muttering, he accepted the bills she gave him. Lindy smiled, sunny and victorious.

"Brava!" Justin applauded her, laughing. "You did a wonderful job. He just paid you the compliment of calling you a robber yourself."

She offered him the peach with a little bow. "For my partner in crime, Signor DiPalma."

"Grazie." He bit into the fruit. "Mmm...delicious, and worth twice the price."

They both laughed, and Justin took her arm.

"Do you suppose two such shady characters should use first names with each other?"

"I would certainly think so...Justin. Most of my friends call me Lindy."

"How lovely. It suits you. And I would very much like us to be friends."

"So would I," Lindy said softly.

It seemed scarcely possible to her that life in the street still swirled so relentlessly. She felt that something markedly important had happened, but she wasn't sure exactly what. They walked in silence for a few moments until Justin cleared his throat.

"The market is closing. Lunchtime."

One by one the awnings disappeared, curling inside themselves, anticipating the siesta. Tables and crates were yanked into the shops, and a few last-minute bargains were struck. The angelus bells began chiming from a nearby churchtower.

"Are you hungry, Lindy?"

"Mmm, yes. This place has given me quite an appetite."

He smiled. "Good. The *ristorante* where we're going is worthy of nothing less."

They started back toward the motor launch. Ever so casually, Justin drew her arm through the crook of his. After two or three awkward steps, Lindy adjusted to his pace, to the occasional jolt of his thigh brushing her hip. When they reached the canal, the full force of the Mediterranean sun hit her and she felt deliciously light-headed.

"Giacomo!" Justin called as they stepped into the boat. "Madame Delphine's."

The old man nodded, and with one motion switched on the ignition and slammed forward the throttle. The pilot of a delivery boat wagged his fist as they cut between him and the *vaporetto*. Lindy glanced back to see the passengers of the water-bus shouting and gesturing. Giacomo seemed oblivious to the protests, weaving and dodging and finally swerving sharply right into a narrow side canal. Just as suddenly as he'd speeded up, he slowed the motorboat to a pious crawl.

Noticing Lindy's dazed expression, Justin patted her hand.

"One must be fearless to navigate the canals," he said solemnly, his eyes belying his tone.

"It's a dangerous game," Lindy nodded.

"Yes, indeed. But what good is anything without the spice of risk?"

She looked to see if he were teasing. His deep green eyes remained steady. Maybe yes, maybe no. Before she could decide, Giacomo interrupted in a cracked and weathered voice.

"Eh, signor."

The engine gave a last gurgle. The motorboat glided alongside an arched doorway leading into one of the buildings lining the canal.

"Here we are, Lindy. Watch your step."

Dubiously, she entered the corridor after him. It was

a cool and rather damp passageway, seeming completely dark, effectively sealed off from the midday sun by thick and ancient stones. She shivered a little.

"Did I understand you correctly? This is the great restaurant you've been promising me?"

"Yes, of course. Well, the back entrance anyway— for special friends of the proprietress only. I think you'll like her."

Lindy was becoming accustomed to the dim light. At first Justin was only a faint outline; now his solid form halted before a wooden planked door. He lifted the lion's-head knocker and rapped three times.

"Madame Delphine is unique," he said, turning and drawing Lindy up beside him. "A Sardinian by birth, a Venetian by temperament and adoption. All sorts of characters dine here, from penniless counts to wealthy crooks, but never any tourists."

"Oh? Then why did we come here?"

He leaned closer, until she could smell the exotic scent of his after shave. "You're a crook, remember? The green-grocer said so. And I am your accomplice."

She laughed, and suddenly the door creaked open. A white-jacketed waiter bowed when he saw Justin, exchanging a few words with him in Italian and summoning them to follow.

He led them to a European caged lift, barred in iron and trimmed in shining brass. Lindy gave a little gasp of delight.

"Oh, I've always wanted to ride in one of these things!"

"Well, step aboard, milady, for the Cook's tour."

With a clang and a jerk, they began to rise. After the ground floor, Lindy could see that they were in a sort of tower and that a marble staircase surrounded their flight. At each floor a small window gave an alluring view: a courtyard, tiled rooftops, a church belfry. They rode all the way to the top, then after a few short steps Justin flung open the final door.

Sunlight splashed over Lindy as she stepped onto the

rooftop terrace. The sand-colored stucco of the house formed three sides and the fourth was open to all Venice, save for a curlicued wrought-iron railing. Big stone tubs with lemon and orange trees, verbena and oleander, made it feel like a garden. In one corner, shaded by a grape arbor, a table was set with a pale green cloth.

"Well, what do you think?"

She turned toward Justin, smiling. "It's wonderful. Really beautiful. But," she added wryly. "It's not your ordinary restaurant."

Justin laughed. "Oh, no. This is Delphine's private terrace. The dining room is often crowded at this hour, and noisy. . . ." He shrugged nonchalantly. "I wanted— that is, I knew we'd have a hard time talking downstairs."

As he seated her at the table and took his place across from her, Lindy gazed at the cerulean sky and smiled. It was so lovely here. Private. Fragrant with the perfume of pink and yellow flowers. Quiet. Only the faint merry bubbling of a tiny fountain nestled in the greenery could be heard.

It was . . . romantic.

She started.

"Is something wrong?"

"Oh . . . no, no. I'm really enjoying the view."

The waiter had quietly appeared with menus and a crystal bowl filled with water for her violets. Thanking him, Lindy hid behind her menu, staring unseeingly at the Italian script. Romantic? Where had *that* come from? Surely not from the woman who professed to want this man as a friend and nothing more. Abruptly, all her nervousness from earlier in the day slipped back to grip her. And just as abruptly, she shook it off. She was being ridiculous.

"Lindy?"

She peeped over the top of the card.

"Mmm?"

"Would you like to order now?"

The waiter's pen was poised to record her every wish. She had no idea what that was.

"Well . . . why don't you order for both of us, Justin? You're the expert on Venetian food."

She welcomed the few moments Justin spoke with the waiter. It gave her a chance to catch her breath, to reprove herself for her foolishness. After all, it wasn't as if he'd brought her there with some idea of conquest. He'd probably had lots of other chances with lots of other women.

Did he bring them here? The setting alone was enough to mellow the toughest resolve.

But not hers, she determined—then was mildly disturbed that the thought gave her no consolation.

"Madame Delphine is busy at the moment," Justin was saying, "The waiter says she promises to join us later. And he recommended the *spaghetti coi pisèlli* and a Valpolicella."

"Sounds intriguing. I don't suppose you're going to tell me what all that is."

"Oh, no. I much prefer pleasant little surprises."

Which, Lindy thought, the day was fast becoming. Justin was less formal then she'd first assumed, or maybe she was merely more relaxed around him than she expected to be.

"You know," she ventured, cupping her chin in her palm, "this is truly a beautiful place—one of those pleasant little surprises you say you're fond of. Do you come here often?"

"Actually, I haven't been here for a long while. Usually my lunch is a quick bite in a small, noisy *trattoria*, and I am nearly always doing business at the same time. So this will be a treat for me."

"But how do you rate all this?" She waved her hand in an arc.

"Oh, a few years ago I did a favor for Delphine, a matter of shoring up the foundation with a few beams and posts." He brushed it lightly away. "Nothing much."

"She must have been . . . very grateful." Lindy knew her smile was a shade too bright, a bit too innocent. Inwardly, she groaned. Stupid, stupid. She sounded coy, and that was one thing she hated. "I mean, to let you use her terrace for . . . for lunches and things."

"Yes, Delphine is quite generous." If he'd found any innuendo in Lindy's words, he gave no notice of it.

She breathed a little easier. It was no business of hers anyway. And besides, Madame Delphine was probably a fossilized old crone.

"Now you tell me, little friend," he smiled. "What do you think of *La Serenissima?*"

It took a moment for Lindy to realize he was speaking not of the proprietress of the restaurant but of the city itself. She thought for a moment.

"I'm totally fascinated with it," she said at last. "It's not like any other place . . . and not just in the obvious way. I mean, most cities have one section, one small area that's old enough and untouched enough to have earned some charm. But here in Venice, that charm is everywhere. There's a timelessness—" She smiled and shook her head. "After a while, I round every corner fully expecting to bump into Tintoretto, on his way to paint another madonna."

"Or a medieval politician plotting the murder of his enemies. One thing you should remember, Lindy: The spirits of both are a part of the spirit of Venice."

Startled, she regarded him curiously. "I thought you loved this city."

"I do. Maybe more so because I know her at her best and worst." He leaned forward, sparks glinting his eyes. "But that's where her beauty comes from. She's lived with the worst of men, it's true, but also with the best. And the good have triumphed! That's what I love. Look around you. What do you see? Those things that have endured—houses, shops, courtyards, churches. Common, everyday magnificence."

Resting back in his chair, Justin gazed across the uneven patchwork of roofs.

"I study the Bellini paintings of the piazza, of the Grand Canal, done five hundred years ago. They look virtually the same today. And I ask myself, do I—does *anyone*—have the right to change something that has endured so many centuries, just for the sake of progress?"

For the first time that day, Lindy really looked at him in profile, penetrating the agreeable social shell surrounding him. His jaw clenched, his eyes slightly narrowed, he seemed almost possessed. She had no doubt that he would fight tirelessly for anything—or anyone—he loved fiercely.

Before she could carry that thought any further, the waiter arrived with their lunch, and Justin became the urbane host once more.

"Now, little friend, your mystery will be solved," he said, filling their glasses with red wine. He tested his and nodded satisfied."Valpolicella. *Bene, bene.*"

The waiter bowed, fussed a moment with the serving cart, and discreetly left.

The wine was light and dry. Lindy sipped contentedly as Justin spread the first course of the meal in front of her, a tempting antipasto of peppers and olives. She'd forgotten how hungry she was.

"It all looks wonderful."

"Wait until you taste it."

"Do you suppose these peppers could have come from the very greengrocer who called me a robber?"

"It's entirely possible."

They both laughed, and Lindy was struck by the change in him. His moods seemed to range from the lightest to the darkest shades. He was a complex man who would not be easy to know intimately—if, she reminded herself sternly, that was something she cared to do.

"You're very quiet, Lindy. Did my little speech about Venice disturb you? Sometimes I get carried away."

"No, no. I was just thinking. You are a man who has very strong feelings about certain things. You're not afraid to jump feet first into controversy, are you?"

"No, I guess I'm not." He considered for a moment, then smiled. "I get suspicious if I'm too content. I need to take a few risks to be happy with myself." Stroking his chin, he regarded her carefully. "I think you're a little like that, too."

"Oh, no," she laughed, "not me. Living dangerously makes me nervous. I've developed into a most cautious person."

"Really? You were a pretty fearless bargainer this morning."

Tipping her wineglass at him, Lindy conceded his point. "A throwback to former times. My fearlessness, as you put it, has gotten me into a lot of trouble at times."

"But you've emerged victorious, no?"

"Well . . . maybe. But not without a few close calls with disaster."

"Ah, my dear Lindy," Justin murmured, "isn't that the essence of life? To win out over those close calls. The exhilaration of it!"

Pausing, she concentrated on her lunch to avoid Justin's intent gaze. When she thought she could face it, she looked up and smiled.

"I can think of nothing more enjoyable than sitting here, with all Venice spread out before me. With great food and drink, and—"

She was horrified to realize she'd almost added, "a handsome man paying attention to me." Their conversation, their whole day, was becoming much too personal.

"—and," she finished lamely, "it would be a crime to waste the rest of the Valpolicella, don't you think?"

Justin blinked, then grasped the bottle with a rueful little grin. "I've neglected my duties, haven't I? Especially so, since in Italy it is a shocking breach of manners to let a guest see the bottom of her glass. Forgive me."

A slender shaft of sunlight pierced the arbor, illuminating the ruby wine he poured.

"Now tell me . . . I want to know more of your impressions of the city. What about St. Mark's?"

Relieved to be on safer ground, Lindy reflected for a moment. "I guess what struck me most was the mosaic work—all those tiny little chips of stone making glorious pictures...."

From a hesitant start, she gradually began easing up, revealing her uncensored feelings about Venice. She found Justin an eager listener, so often nodding in agreement with what she said. Long after the last forkful of spaghetti was eaten and the final drop of wine swallowed, they still talked and wondered aloud about the city's past.

"Mi dispiace," a gentle feminine voice crooned. Lindy looked toward the doorway just as a tall, graceful figure in a white-and-gold caftan swept through. *"Mi dispiace.* I am sorry I am so late to greet you. Giustino ... what miracle pulled you from your work?"

Justin cleared his throat behind his fist, raising an eyebrow at the speaker. "I'd like you to meet my friend, Melinda Thorne."

A smile softened the bold features of Madame Delphine. Everything about her suggested nobility, from the broad expanse of her brow and her upswept black hair to her regal carriage. With a sinking feeling, Lindy realized that the "fossilized old crone" had not yet seen her fortieth birthday—and that she was a strikingly handsome woman.

"... so many people today," she was saying. "I could not get away sooner."

"Perfectly understandable, madame. Besides, my friend and I had a lovely lunch."

Lindy smiled. Yes ... lovely.

"It was, Madame. Everything ... was delicious."

"Bene, bene. But now you must go?"

Justin was pulling back her chair, and Lindy stood, knocking her straw clutch to the floor and scattering the contents.

"Oh, excuse me, Lindy——"

"No, no. My fault. I should have grabbed it or something...."

She bit her lip before anything more gauche could escape. As she scraped up her belongings, Lindy was sure she was blushing redder than a pomegranate. And she was just as sure that Madame Delphine was fully composed, watching her nearly sprawled on the terrace floor, chasing after her lipstick and spare change.

Scrambling to her feet, squeezing her purse tightly against her body, she made an attempt to laugh it off. "Well...thanks for such a delicious meal. Everything was...delicious." Oh God, get me out of here, she thought frantically.

"I am so happy you enjoyed it," Madame Delphine said, lightly taking her hand. Her scent was a potpourri of spices. "Tell Giustino to bring you again, *si?*"

Lindy nodded, all the while wondering if he still thought she was fit to escort in public. He kissed Madame Delphine on both cheeks, and they exchanged a few parting words in Italian before descending in the antique elevator.

As she and Justin passed through the dark corridor and stepped back into Giacomo's boat, Lindy sighed deeply. She realized she'd been holding her breath for a long time.

Justin handed her the bouquet she'd forgotten at the table.

"Would you like to know where we're going now?"

She clutched the violets gratefully. "Yes. Where are we going?"

"I won't tell you. It's another one of my pleasant surprises."

She stared at him for a second, then broke into a merry smile. "I'm ready for anything."

They reached the little shop only after a winding boat ride and a walk along a mazelike trail through short alleys. The window with its dark green awning gave no clue to the merchandise inside. The words, *Casa Santino,* were etched on the glass. A tinkling bell announced their entrance. It took a few minutes for Lindy's eyes to adjust to the muted light in the shop. Then she swiveled slowly, her delight growing.

The walls were lined with tiered display cases that reached to the ceiling. On every shelf stood small objects—vases and bowls, figures of animals and people, trees and flowers. And every one was made of jewel-bright glass.

A small, thin man with a black mustache to match brushed through a curtain in the rear, wiping his hands on a napkin. At the sight of Justin, he perked up and grinned, slipping into his suit jacket and offering his hand. Justin spoke a few phrases, and the man bowed, clicking his heels in the direction of each of them as he stepped aside.

"Signor Santino comes from a long line of Murano craftsmen," Justin told Lindy. "All these are his creations."

Santino snapped a switch, and the backs of the display cases glowed with soft light. The colors leaped to life; clear, brilliant colors of emerald and garnet and gold.

"Oh," Lindy breathed, "how beautiful!"

Her gaze swept from a figurine the hue of flame to a fragile bluebird and finally to a graceful sailboat. She moved closer, her eyes gleaming.

As if reading her thoughts, Santino slid open the display and reverently lifted the boat. He placed it in her hands. Lindy held it up carefully to the light. The colors were perfectly blended—deep cobalt for the hull shading into turquoise and green for the sail.

"You like it?" Justin asked behind her.

"I love it! I've been sailing since I was a child. Some of my happiest . . . Oh, this is the most exquisite piece I've ever seen."

"Then you must have it. Signor Santino?" He removed his wallet.

The shop owner gently took the boat from her and began wrapping it.

"I couldn't let you buy it for me," Lindy protested.

"I'm merely returning the gift you gave me this morning," Justin replied, smiling. "Remember the peach?"

"Oh, but the two are hardly of the same value. The peach cost only pennies, and this . . . why, this is a work of art!"

"My dear Lindy," Justin said softly, "gifts should be measured by the joy they bring. The two are very much the same value."

He picked up the string-tied package and took her arm. She stared at him wordlessly as they left the shop.

Oh, he shouldn't have said that, Lindy thought, feeling her vow not to become involved with him shattering like the most delicate Murano glass.

"I've so many more places to show you," he was saying. "I know you'll love them. There's Piero's, he makes beads. And——"

"Justin," she interrupted. Her head was suddenly swimming and slightly aching. "I—I think I'm a little tired . . . not used to these long adventures." She smiled a little to let him know she was not displeased with him. "Could we call it a day now?"

"Of course, of course," he said, a note of apology in his voice.

The journey back to her hotel was mostly silent. Having come so close to him, Lindy could think of nothing to say that wasn't either trite or asinine. Justin seemed pensive, but not disturbed or angry. She found herself looking forward to the coolness of her room, and yet she felt a certain sadness that their day was ending—by her own request, no less.

"Here we are," Justin said at last, and she looked up to see the imposing facade of the Doges' Palace and the Royal Danieli Hotel. He helped her out of the *motoscafo* and walked her to the lobby.

"Thank you for a delightful day," he said rather formally.

"Oh, Justin," she said, touching his arm. "I want you to know I really did have a marvelous time. Everything was wonderful—the market, the shops, the lunch. And I love my sailboat."

His smile relaxed measurably. "I'm glad." He kissed her hand with a soft caress. "Perhaps we can do it again sometime."

"Perhaps . . ."

He turned and began walking away, his back so straight, his gait so smooth. Lindy opened her mouth to call to him, but no words seemed appropriate.

Just as she was about to leave, he turned and spoke her name. "Lindy——" He stepped five paces closer to her. "I have a full schedule of work in the next few days.... But if I can take an afternoon off next week, will you go sailing in the lagoon with me?"

In a split second, all Lindy's rationales battled. Yes, go—No, don't.

"I'd love to," she answered.

Justin beamed. "Good. I'll call you."

"Yes. *Arrivederci*."

"No, my little friend. *Ciao*."

With a wave, he was off. Lindy couldn't swear to it, but his stride seemed lighter, swifter this time. As she moved toward the elevator, her own feet seemed to fly.

- 5 -

HER ROOM FELT cool and tranquil, a welcome contrast
to the activity of the morning. Lindy drew a deep bath
and seasoned it with honeysuckle-scented oil. She
climbed in and let the soothing water coax her into relaxing.

Celine had left a message:

Went shopping. Back soon to hear all the JUICY
details!

Love,
C.

In spite of herself, Lindy sighed, grateful to have a
few moments alone to sort out those details, knowing
her sister would consider them very juicy indeed. Maybe
it would be best to play everything down, to tell Celine
it had been nice enough...slightly boring...ordinary.

Groaning, she patted her temples with a warm cloth.

Her sister would sooner believe the sky was falling. No, she'd have to come closer to the truth...which was...

...that she'd just spent an exceedingly pleasurable day. With a most fascinating person. The fact that he was a charming and good-looking man had very little to do with it.

Sure. Whatever you say, Henny Penny.

Wearily, Lindy lathered up her skin and rinsed away the soapy bubbles. Sliding down in the water until she was submerged to her chin, she stared unseeingly at the carved ceiling. Why was she trying so desperately to fool herself? She'd had a marvelous day with Justin. And when was the last time she'd truly enjoyed herself with a man? It had to have been ages ago, right after she and Blair were married.

Ah, yes, that was it, wasn't it? Didn't an old adage say that history repeats itself? Her dates with Blair had been just as much fun at first. And for a while after the wedding, on their extended honeymoon, nearly every day had been as entertaining and happy. The entire Caribbean was at their disposal. They spent weeks in secluded beach-front cottages, then flew into San Juan or Barbados for some exhilarating night life. When one island paradise became too familiar, they hopscotched to another. It appeared to be an idyllic life, and more than once, Lindy had pinched herself to be sure it was real.

So when had everything started to go wrong? That question had haunted Lindy when her marriage had crumbled. Sometime in the second year? By that time they had settled in New York City, in a spacious and airy town house. Blair had presented her with a sheaf of charge cards and carte blanche to decorate herself and the apartment any way she chose. Every day was Christmas, and they were invited to a different cocktail party every night. For weeks on end, Lindy's main meal of the day consisted of vodka martinis and hot hors d'oeuvres.

Blair went to his father's office three or four days a week. Every other month he'd come home at lunch flapping airline tickets. And by suppertime, they were in Acapulco or Rio or St. Tropez.

So when was it that the excitement had begun to tarnish? When she'd noticed how predictable their lives, their crowd had become? They were all in a rut, and no matter how much they slicked it with suntan oil and doused it with Courvoisier and lined it with Givenchys, it was still a rut. She began to crave a normal life. She wanted to have a baby.

"So soon?" Blair was surprised when she told him. "Darling, think how that would tie you down. The Stanfords are renting a whole island this winter, remember? And next year we're seriously thinking about that Far East cruise. You know you couldn't bear to miss that."

"To tell you the truth, Blair, I could happily give up some of this gadding about that we do. There are some hotels that I actually know more intimately than my own home." At the sight of his frown, she touched his arm and smiled weakly. "Sooner or later we'll go to one party too many, and our poor livers will go on strike."

"Of course, darling. That's why on the eighth day, God created spas. If you're feeling a little tired, we could book you into one. Matter of fact, the Worthingtons are going——"

For the first time, she became exasperated with him. "Blair, that's not what I mean. I want us to be a real family. With a home that we *live* in, and children—"

He kissed her. "All right, if it means so much to you, *mein* little *hausfrau*. We'll get cracking next spring."

But spring budded and bloomed into summer, and Blair had one excuse after another. Gradually, Lindy retreated from their manic social schedule, and decided she'd rather stay home alone than hear the latest installment in their friend Gwen's divorce case.

That first evening they each felt awkward about her staying home and his leaving, but that eased with time and practice. Lindy enrolled in Columbia University to complete her degree. She switched her major to English literature to give herself an excuse to curl up with books on the nights Blair was out . . . which was almost every night.

Later, she realized she'd been burying her head in the works of Thomas Hardy so she wouldn't have to face the antics of her husband. More than once Blair stumbled in at breakfast, his impeccable suit rumpled, a strange perfume clinging to his shirt. Finally, she couldn't ignore it any longer.

"Well, is Gwen feeling better about her divorce?"

"Gwen? How . . . did you——"

"Oh, some of our *friends* were only too happy to let me in on it. They felt *so sorry* for me. Oh, yes, so sorry that their eyes were gleaming and their fangs were dripping——"

"Melinda, please don't cry."

"I can't help it; I was so humiliated. . . ."

"Melinda . . . dear . . . I thought you understood about these things. Believe me, darling, it's just a little kindness to a good friend. It doesn't have anything to do with us. I still love you and want you to be my wife."

She stared at him, incredulous. "What do you mean, it doesn't have anything to do with us? We're married, you're my husband, you're supposed to be faithful to me!"

"I am . . . emotionally, and that's the way that counts. Come on, darling. It's not the Dark Ages. I thought you understood. . . . I am sorry, my dear."

"Oh God, Blair . . . so am I."

He had shaken her to her soul. She wasn't sophisticated enough for him, or desirable enough. Her self-esteem plummeted, and all she could think of doing was to hold onto the part of him that still loved her.

And then had come that fateful day. She remembered it so clearly. It was one of those rare April afternoons when the sky was a shiny blue and the air spanking clean.

She'd spent the morning at Elizabeth Arden's, and she was going to surprise Blair with a picnic lunch and tickets to Aruba—a mad stab at saving their marriage.

The secretary had gone to lunch, and the door to Blair's office stood ajar. She started to go in, but hearing the mumble of voices, she sat in the anteroom, nervously checking her new hairdo.

". . . part of the agreement, young man. I told you the balance of your trust would come to you only when I was good and sure you had settled down."

"I know that, Grandmother. I've been married for——"

"Don't try to fool me, young man. You're very dear to me . . . so like your grandfather . . . but I won't be charmed by your evasions. You may have married, but you certainly haven't settled down. Now if you want the quarterly installment on that trust, you'd better start staying home with your wife."

"Very well, Grandmother. I'll be the model husband. . . ."

Lindy fled, tears melting her perfect makeup. Her marriage had been nothing more than a business deal, collateral for Blair's trust fund. He had no love for her, and the only reason to stay married had suddenly dissolved. She filed for divorce the same week.

Lindy came out of her reverie with a start, and was amazed to realize that her eyes were bordered with tears. It was not that she still felt anything for Blair; it was more like an old wound that turned achy on a rainy day.

Still, she couldn't help remembering how devastated she'd been, and that it had all begun with a few casual dates.

"But this isn't the same," she whispered, gently rippling the bath water with her fingers. "I'm a whole different person now. My eyes are wide open, and I know how to put on the skids when I have to."

Justin DiPalma was different too. He was as fervent

as Blair had been blasé. And why shouldn't she have some fun? There was nothing wrong with that.

Nothing at all, she insisted silently, hopping out of the tub and vigorously toweling herself dry. She slipped into an ivory silk wrapper and was patting moisturizing cream on her face when there came an eager knock on the connecting door.

"Lindy? It's me."

"Hi, Celine. Come on in."

Balancing a cocktail glass in each hand, Celine entered and beelined for the chaise longue. She kicked off her shoes and collapsed onto the chaise, sloshing a little liquid on the carpet.

"Here, I brought you a martini. Now tell me everything!"

Shaking her head, Lindy laughed. "If you had a subtle bone in your body, you'd be dangerous." She sat opposite her sister, waving away the drink. "You know I hate those things."

Celine rolled her eyes. "Oh, Lord, does that mean I'm going to need both of them?"

"Sister dear——"

"All right, all right. Just don't keep me in suspense any longer. Tell me!"

"We had a lovely day," Lindy said calmly. "We went to the Rialto markets, had lunch, and stopped in a glass shop. It was...pleasant. That's all."

Martini halfway to her lips, Celine stared. "That's all? What about *him?* What's he like? Come on...give."

"What do you want me to say? He's a nice guy."

"A nice guy." Celine sniffed. "And Michelangelo was a nice painter....Don't frown at me, kiddo. What's he like? Was he as charming as he was yesterday at lunch? Did he kiss your hand again? Is he married?"

"Why...I don't know." Lindy reflected a moment, remembering his strong, lean fingers raised in bargaining, pouring wine, helping her into the boat. "He wasn't wearing a ring."

"Oh, shoot. That doesn't mean a thing, especially in Italy. What do you think? Did he *sound* married?"

Lindy jumped up, exasperated. "I don't know, Celine. What does *married* sound like? I was married to Blair for four years, and nobody ever thought he sounded like it. Besides, what does it matter if Justin is or isn't? It was a simple date, not a formal engagement." Crossing her arms, she wandered restlessly across the room.

"You know I can't stand to be pressured. Why do you keep pushing me just to satisfy your curiosity?"

Celine reproached her with wounded eyes. "You know that's not it," she said softly. "I care about you. I know how unhappy you've been. Here we are in Venice, for heaven's sake . . . and, honey, you've got to admit"—she waited until Lindy was facing her—"he is one gorgeous man!"

Recognizing defeat when she saw it, Lindy sighed. She came toward her sister and dropped a kiss on her cheek with a little laugh. "You're right. He *is* gorgeous . . . and I know you care about me. I couldn't have made it through these last couple of years without your support. Since Mother died, you've even sort of taken her place."

"Right. And as a good mother, I want to know all about the man you're seeing."

"Celine, you're incorrigible." Groaning good-naturedly, Lindy lolled on the bed, leaning her chin on her fist. "Okay. Let me think . . ." She paused for a while, gathering random impressions and trying to shape them into Justin.

"He's fun to be with. He knows all kinds of interesting, out-of-the-way places. . . . He must be something of a digger, an explorer, because these aren't places you'd find by chance. He notices little details, and they matter to him. He is charming, but it's very natural. And believe me, I've seen enough of the fake to know the difference."

"He sounds divine!"

"The fascinating thing about him," Lindy said thoughtfully, talking to herself now, "is that he is a much more complex person than he seems. At first, I saw mostly his European side, the courtly and continental part. Which was really fun—distant, but comfortable. Then the American strain came out in him; he was more relaxed, friendly, joking with me.... We had a good time together."

She hesitated and her brow furrowed slightly. "But I think that there is a deeper part of him—a part he rarely shows anyone—and I think that's the *real* Justin. I only caught glimpses of him like that.... I don't really know how to describe it.... sort of intense and driven, passionate about the things that matter to him. It made me wonder if—" She stopped herself and looked at Celine, whose eyes were shining.

Lindy sat up and stretched. "I guess that's all I know about him. He doesn't give many pieces of himself away."

Celine leaned back in the chaise dreamily. "Mystery is so sexy."

"Now Celine, don't start that again. He's a good companion. We could probably be great pals, but I am not interested in him in any other way."

"For a girl who is not interested," Celine commented slyly, "you sure did a lot of probing into what makes him tick."

Lindy brushed her words away, moving to the dressing table and nervously flicking at her curls with a comb. "Force of habit. Until not too long ago, I made my living at the radio station that way, remember?"

"Uh-huh. So, are you going out with him again?"

"Well...yes. We're going sailing next week."

Unconsciously, she glanced at the bureau where the Murano sailboat rested, its vibrant colors muted in the dim light. Too late, she realized that Celine's gaze had followed hers. Celine leaped up to get a better look at it.

"Melinda! How beautiful! Oh, don't tell me he gave

this to you. It's simply stunning. Well, I can't say that I'm surprised. Yesterday, watching him with you at lunch, I just knew it. I told Steven later, 'That man definitely likes my sister.' I could just tell. What a heavenly present. He must have excellent taste."

Lindy was glad that the bunch of violets was safely out of sight in the bathroom, languishing in the drinking glass, vulnerable but still lovely. Somehow, she felt it was a gift even more intimate than the sailboat.

"... I cannot wait," Celine was saying, "until tomorrow evening, the *Patria Grande* cocktail reception. Remember how he finagled an invitation from Steven? I'll bet it was just so he could see you again. Isn't it incredible?"

Lindy bit her lip pensively. The reception—she'd forgotten all about it. She would see him much sooner than she'd expected. A tiny glow cheered her.

She only hoped Justin hadn't forgotten.

The party was well underway by the time they arrived. Lindy paused in the doorway, getting her bearings.

The private room of the Doges' Palace was large, with vaulted ceilings corniced in gold. It gleamed of polished wood and marble. Clusters of guests were engaging in polite conversations, punctuated by the well-bred tinkle of an occasional ice cube and women's laughter. Beside the buffet table, a string quartet played Vivaldi.

"Lindy, come *on*." Celine was trying to curb her excitement, as befitted the wife of the important American consultant. Her eyes betrayed her. "Look at that man with all the medals on his chest. I'll bet he's a general or something. Maybe he's royalty! Can you imagine being introduced to a prince?"

The portly man bowed to them from across the room, twitching his mustache at them. They began to follow Steven to the reception line.

"Don't get your hopes up, Celine," Lindy said dryly. "He probably bought those medals at a flea market."

"Really, Lindy ... And isn't that woman with him the

automotive heiress? She must have half the diamonds in Europe around her neck!"

"Don't be too impressed. Wearing a bunch of ribbons—or diamonds, for that matter—doesn't automatically make a person wonderful or interesting. Or even rich."

"Well, that may be so. But I'll tell you one thing: I can spot a designer dress at a hundred paces. And you and I are the only females in this room who aren't wearing one."

Lindy knew she was right. As they waited in the reception line, pearls at her throat, she wondered if she'd made a mistake in leaving her best clothes at home. Remnants of her marriage, she hardly ever wore them. Venetians, it seemed, loved to show off their finery.

She shrugged, dismissing the thought. Her beige silk dress swished comfortingly when she walked, and she knew the open-toed high heels set off her slender legs becomingly. Besides, who was she trying to impress?

"I don't see him yet," Celine confided in a low tone.

"Who?"

"Who? That nice-guy painter, Michelangelo. Who, indeed."

"Celine . . ."

"Hah! Caught you this time. I saw you looking for him too."

"Shh. Turn around, Steven's next."

They passed through the line in a repetitious jumble of *buona sera*'s and how-do-you-do's, being presented to various politicians and sundry minor nobility. After the last handshake, a passing waiter offered them glasses of sparkling wine.

"Ah, my friends," a voice chuckled behind them. "So good you are here."

Lindy turned, only to find herself looking over the balding head of Ugo Gilberti. He rocked forward on the balls of his feet, kissing her hand with a swoop. "My dear," he said fervently, his eyes half shut.

Before Lindy could close her mouth and reply, he had switched his ministrations to Celine, and then finally gotten around to Steven. "Good evening, Signor Marsh. Please, most charming and delightful ladies, excuse us."

As he led Steven toward an eager group of business-men, the two sisters looked at each other and laughed.

"He certainly is direct," Celine noted.

The reception line had broken ranks, and small de-tachments of those they had met briefly came by to chat with the two sisters. Lindy's glass was whisked away, replaced by a fresh one, and one handsome gentleman, who was either the mayor or an army official, would not let her speak a word until she had sampled the lavish buffet.

She was beginning to relax and enjoy the friendly courtesy when she noticed a pale-haired woman who looked familiar at the other end of the long table. It took a few minutes' search of her memory to recall that they'd met in St. Croix—or was it Biarritz?—two or three years ago. Her name was Bobo or Bibi, something like that, Lindy thought. She was a dedicated rider on the inter-national merry-go-round.

The woman looked up, seeming rather bored. Her gaze casually brushing Lindy, she started to amble down the line.

Oh, no, Lindy groaned inwardly. She was going to have to talk to her. She wondered if she knew about. . . . oh, God, what if she was one of Blair's women?

Drawing a deep breath, she braced herself, but the sleek blonde sailed obliviously by. Lindy sipped her wine, relieved. Yet that glimpse of the painful past had taken some of the glitter out of the evening.

"Enough of that," she scolded herself under her breath.

"Did you say something, dear?"

"No . . . ah . . . just that I've had enough wine for the moment."

"Oh, well, Signor Vanelli was telling me about a big

festival coming up next week. The Re—re——"

"*Redentore, signora,* the largest feast of the summer. Perhaps you..."

The gentleman went on and on, but suddenly Lindy was no longer aware of what he was saying. She couldn't point to anything specific she'd seen or heard, but something pulled her attention to the center of the chandelier-lit room. Her heart gave an irregular thump.

Justin had arrived. He stood in a small knot of people, towering over most of them, smiling a bit and nodding. Slowly, purposefully, he glanced up, and Lindy started, because it was as if he felt her eyes on him. Mouthing his apologies, he extricated himself and moved toward her.

"Hello," he said, lightly pressing her hands between his.

"Hi."

He had a way of leaving her speechless. She wished she could think of something clever to say, but no words came to her.

"Lindy, you look lovely," he said softly, still holding her hands.

She swallowed. "Thank you. I'm...glad you came."

"Did you think I wouldn't? After I practically twisted your brother-in-law's arm for an invitation?"

"Well," she laughed, "I didn't think about it yesterday."

"Neither did I. I guess I was having too good a time."

His grin flashed briefly, so dazzling against his olive skin. Lindy couldn't help but notice how beautifully his soft gray suit fit and how the light bouncing off the chandelier gleamed in his ebony hair.

"Have you any idea," Justin was saying, "of what a stir we are making? These gentlemen are properly aghast that the wolf has not only invaded their pasture, but is monopolizing the prize lamb."

"Lamb? None of you has ever seen me when I'm good and mad."

"No"—Justin's eyes glowed for a second before he

smiled—"but I can imagine it."

Before she could answer or even think about what he meant, Steven approached with Gilberti reluctantly in tow.

"Nice to see you again, DiPalma."

"Thank you, Mr. Marsh. Gilberti..."

"Signor." The small man shook Justin's hand stiffly. "It is a surprise most entirely that I see you here."

"Well, Mr. Marsh was good enough to invite me."

Steven nodded. "You don't mind, do you? I mean, in the interest of hearing both sides to the question of Venice's future."

"No, *no*." Gilberti drew himself up until he was level with Justin's breast pocket. "I am one-hundred-percent confident of my position."

The difference in their sizes was creating a belligerence in Gilberti, Lindy noticed. The man was ready for combat.

"Why don't we sit down?" Justin suggested. "The *signorina* will be more comfortable that way."

As he grasped her elbow and guided them toward a grouping of settees, Lindy glanced at his well-defined profile. Though his consideration of her was a small, seemingly casual gesture he'd made to disarm Gilberti, it was one she'd remember...another facet of this most fascinating man.

The rose-colored damask couches were set at right angles to each other. Steven and Gilberti took the one Justin indicated; he sat beside Lindy on the other. She busied herself crossing her legs and straightening her skirt to disguise the tingle of happiness she felt.

She was being ridiculous again, she told herself. He probably only wanted to see those two head-on. Just sitting next to her didn't mean a thing.

But close enough so that he could have put his arm around her if he wanted? Or if she had wanted him to. His thigh touched hers, jumbling her thoughts and putting a flush in her cheeks.

Lindy flagged a waiter and snatched a glass of wine

from his tray, telling herself that the warmth of the room was making her thirsty.

"I must explain one thing," Gilberti was saying, waving a plump finger in the air. "We are not the barbarians like sometimes your people say, DiPalma. We appreciate beauty. For an example, I say never would we tear down this magnificent *palazzo*."

"Millions would thank you for that," Justin replied dryly, and as Gilberti bristled, he added, "Seriously, Ugo, what would *Patria Grande* do with it?"

The Italian's brown eyes shone. "Ah, we have a most good plan." Not to miss a chance to influence the American consultant, he addressed Steven. "You see, once all *Venezia* was ruled from this very place. The most great merchant state, that was *Venezia!* Many ships, much trade, a prosperous port city, that was *Venezia.*"

He leaned forward, nearly popping his suit buttons. "Such days can be again, Signor Marsh. Many rooms in this *palazzo* are not in use, even for visitors. Fine quarters for a new port office!"

"What remodeling would have to be done?" Justin asked quietly.

"Nessuno," Gilberti insisted, chins high with triumph. "None."

Nodding, Justin sat back. Only the random drumming of his fingertips on the settee betrayed his impatience. "You mean none until the filing cabinets scratch centuries-old marble floors; or until stone walls are too cold in the winter, and you panel them or lower the ceiling or——"

Gilberti's round face was reddening in a way that reminded Lindy of Ed, her old boss. "Signor, there is only one way to greatness. That is to make progress"— he spiraled his finger upward—"progress, DiPalma. *È cosi. Finito!*"

The tension crackled between them. Justin was very still, his eyes narrow. "The greatness of Venice, *signor,* is that so far she has been able to preserve the greatness of her past. We have no right to destroy it in the name of progress. If you want to modernize a city, to develop a port, go across the lagoon to the mainland, to Mestre. It could use a little progress. But for God's sake, leave Venice alone."

Throwing up his hands, Gilberti sighed. "Signor Marsh," he implored, "as a man of century twenty, please tell what is in your mind."

Steven cleared his throat and put on his official-business frown. "Well, of course, I need to study the situation further...but some things seem obvious. There are buildings here that have very unstable foundations. They should be razed——"

"Oh, Steven!" Lindy groaned. "How can you even suggest such a thing? This gorgeous city, these wonderful old houses. Surely there are things you can do, ways of saving—"

Abruptly, she stopped. All three pairs of eyes were on her. Steven's disapproving, Gilberti's incredulous; Justin's...admiring? She wasn't sure, but unable to hold his gaze, she concentrated on rubbing the stem of her wineglass between her fingers.

"Excuse me for speaking out of turn," she murmured.

"Actually, you're quite right," Justin said smoothly, filling the awkward gap. "As a matter of fact, I've done some restoration myself. On the Rio di Carmini, I just completed..."

Lindy drained the last of her wine and sat back almost numb. Whatever had possessed her to explode like that? Hadn't she learned her lesson about jumping into causes that didn't concern her? It simply was not worth it to get so involved in things she ultimately had no control over.

"Ah, there you are, Giustino. Where have you been hiding?"

Lindy looked up. The low, sultry voice came from a stunning, sloe-eyed woman who stood before them. As the men rose deferentially, Lindy sneaked a glance at "Giustino." His smile was genial.

"Buona sera. May I present Miss Melinda Thorne, Mr. Steven Marsh, Signor Ugo Gilberti? And this is Vittoria, Contessa D'Alente."

The *contessa* dropped a perfunctory nod at Lindy and then lit up a megawatt smile for the gentlemen. "I hope I am not interrupting..." The men protested her apology.

Moving to stand between Justin and Lindy, she said over her shoulder, "You don't mind, do you, dear? I haven't seen this bad boy for such a long time. Work, work, work. He never has time for me."

Without waiting for a reply, she slipped down on the settee, gently squeezing Lindy into the corner. When the men were seated, Vittoria patted her coiled black chignon with scarlet-tipped fingers.

"I think you don't like me anymore," she said with a measured pout. "I haven't seen you for months, not since the *Bell'Italia* fund-raising ball in *Roma.*"

"My office takes messages, if you had wanted to contact me," Justin answered evenly.

She waved his words away. "It's too late. Someone else inspected the *palazzo* just last week. It is hopeless, it will be torn down later this summer."

"Hopeless?" Remembering his manners, Justin hastily explained their conversation to the others present. "The *contessa*'s home here in Venice is in need of extensive repair. But surely, Vittoria, not hopeless."

She gazed at him playfully through a fringe of dark lashes. "Then convince me otherwise." The invitation in her voice was clear and specific.

"This is...er...hardly the place." For the first time, Justin sounded a bit annoyed.

"No, no," Vittoria argued. "Signor Tommaso is just over there. Come talk to him. Your friends will excuse you, won't they? Of course. It was indeed a pleasure meeting all of you."

Without a backward glance, she was hauling him away. Justin hesitated a moment, beginning to resist. When it was obvious that the headstrong *contessa* would make a scene if he refused, he turned to Lindy, his gold-flecked eyes apologetic.

"This won't take long, I promise. I'll be right back."

"Sure . . . Take your time."

"A handsome woman," Steven said as they melted into the crowd. "Now Signor Gilberti, I'd like——"

"Steven," Lindy cut in, gathering up her handbag, "I'm getting a crushing headache. Would you please explain to Celine and give my thanks to our hosts? I'm going back to the hotel."

"By yourself?" Her brother-in-law frowned. "I don't know . . ."

"Oh, for heaven's sake, it's just next door. I'll be fine. Goodnight, signor."

Before either could reply, she was halfway to the door. She hurried down the staircase, and only when she could breathe the sweet air of early evening did she slow down.

"Oh, Giustino," she muttered mockingly, "you've been such a bad boy."

Her head was beginning to throb in earnest, and there was a sourness in the pit of her stomach. It's those damn cocktail parties, she told herself, remembering why she'd quit going to them in the first place.

Coming to a halt on the steps of the Riva degli Schiavoni, she leaned on the railing and gazed out over the Basin of St. Mark. The lavender sunset had shaded the water a hazy purple. Cigarette-thin gondolas bobbed at their moorings.

As she had mocked Vittoria, an internal voice nagged at her. "Jealous?"

No, she thought—anything but that, *please*. It was such an unreasonable feeling, having no regard for her desire to chase it away. Senseless, and sickeningly familiar.

How was that woman connected to Justin? She'd spoken so intimately to him. Was it because of what they had been to each other, or because of what the slinky *contessa* hoped they would be? One was as bad as the other. Lindy was willing to bet that Vittoria didn't get much rejection.

Oh stop it! she scolded herself mentally. He's just a friend, remember? It's no concern of yours——

She jumped as she felt a light touch on her arm.

"I'm sorry I had to leave you like that," Justin murmured beside her. "The *contessa* can be so insistent. . . ."

"Oh." Lindy tried to recover her poise, to wipe away what she knew was a glum expression. "That's okay. It was a business meeting; you're expected to talk . . . business."

"Something like that." Justin smiled, following the cast of her eyes to the swaying gondolas. "Say, how about a ride? I'll take you home in style."

She pointed to her left, to the Hotel Danieli. "I'm practically on my front porch now."

"Oh, come on. We'll take the long way home."

Her first instinct was to disappear quickly, before he could sense that irrational jealousy. But he *had* left the party to follow her only minutes after she had gone. And she was beyond playing schoolgirl games, making him beg for forgiveness. That was probably one of Vittoria's specialties.

"All right."

As they descended the steps, Justin took her hand. The warmth of it, the electricity his touch provoked, left Lindy feeling almost dizzy. A tenor aria from a passing gondolier floated on the deepening shadows. Justin pulled her next to him as they waited quayside for a boat, releasing her hand and putting his arm around her shoulder. Without thinking, Lindy leaned lightly into him, tilting her face toward his.

For a moment, their eyes locked and Lindy felt sure she'd stopped breathing. As if powerless against a magnetic force, she drew closer to him. Closer . . . closer . . . Her eyes fluttered shut.

"*Eh, signor.* You want ride or no?"

The gondolier's growl was like a splash of icy water

from the canal. Lindy pulled back, her breath coming in staccato gasps, her heart pounding in counterpoint.

"Uh...uh..." Justin's voice was barely more than a croak, and he cleared his throat nervously. "I think not. We'll walk."

Stiffly, Lindy began pacing off the few mile-long steps to the hotel. He matched her stride, a wall of space separating them. Lindy dared only one peek at his face, swiftly looking away at the sight of his scowl.

"I...I'll call you," he said at the entrance to the lobby.

"Oh...fine." Lindy managed to whisper.

- 6 -

THERE WAS ONLY one open table at the sidewalk *trattoria*. The waiter seated Lindy with a flourish and a wiggle of his eyebrows, as if awarding her the best spot on the square in appreciation of her beauty. She barely noticed, wanting only a shady place to settle in and a drink to sip.

"A Galliano and two orange sodas," she muttered, too tired to think about the Italian translation.

As the waiter threaded his way inside, she lifted her sunglasses. "Now where—oh, there you are."

Todd and Tammy came racing across the *piazza* and scraped back their chairs before flopping down. Lindy flinched and dropped the glasses over her eyes again.

"Not so loud, kids. Auntie has a headache."

"You said that yesterday," Tammy reminded her, twirling a strand of blonde hair around her finger.

"Yeah," Todd chimed in. "And Mom didn't believe

you. She told Dad, 'Something must have happened Saturday night. Now what was it?' and he said, 'I don't know. Why don't you ask her?' and Mom said, 'I did, but she wouldn't tell me and——'"

"Here's your soda, Todd. Drink up."

She just needed an anonymous corner where she didn't have to explain anything or make conversation or even think . . . especially not think.

"Okay, Aunt Lindy, let's go."

"We just got here."

"Yeah, but we're done."

Glancing up at the bright little faces with orange half-moons over their upper lips, she had to smile.

"Tell you what"—she scanned the broad *piazza* with its bordering circle of cafés—"there are some kids kicking a ball around over there. I bet they'd let you play if you——"

"Yeah, let's go!"

They scampered off on sturdy legs, and she watched them almost with envy. There was such freedom in their galloping strides. They didn't have to analyze every step for potential pitfalls.

A lithe gray cat nudged her ankles and then, as if sensing her mood, skittered off. From the peeling Renaissance church on the corner came the rich tone of the vesper bell. Six o'clock. Nobody in the square paid attention or seemed to care about it. Lindy tasted the anise liqueur. It wasn't something she'd usually order, but today the thick sweetness of it soothed a throat and a temper scratchy from air-conditioning.

She'd spent all of the day before in her room, making work for herself. After she'd washed her hair and polished her nails, after she'd cleaned out her purse and balanced her checkbook and taken a nap, the evening still stretched before her. She curled up in bed with a novel she'd been wanting to read, but the words had melted into the pages, and all she could see was Justin's face as he bent nearer and nearer . . .

Lindy leaned back in her chair, suppressing a sigh.

It had been the same for two days. The harder she tried to ignore the truth, the more it persisted.

Draining the last of the Galliano, she signaled for another. High time she faced it: Her immunity wasn't so strong. It was not as if she'd lost control on the *riva;* she *had* stepped away before he could kiss her... but she really hadn't wanted to. If it hadn't been for that intrusive gondolier...

All her "platonic" intentions concerning Justin had evaporated in the filmy twilight. She *was* attracted to him, and in ways that alternately thrilled and frightened her. A little bit like she'd felt about——

Stop it, she told herself. Stop comparing Blair and Justin. They're not anything alike—except that women found them both deliciously appealing.

Inwardly, Lindy groaned. She'd wandered through yesterday and today half in a daze, one minute furious with Justin for trying to kiss her, the next furious with herself for pulling away. It was an altogether exhausting experience.

A fresh drink sat in front of her, and she hadn't even seen anyone bring it. She took a few quick sips and called for the bill, ignoring the waiter's hopeful winks.

"Todd, Tammy, let's go!"

Celine should be about ready for her brood. She'd asked Lindy to occupy them while she dressed for a dinner meeting. Steven was speaking to some civic club, and Celine was more nervous than he was.

"Oh, you're back! How do I look? Is this dress okay? My hair didn't come out right. It wants to flip up instead of turn under. I can't——"

"Here, let me." Lindy sat her sister down in front of the mirror and began brushing, rolling the ends under as she went. "There. How's that?"

Celine sighed in relief. "Much better. Thanks. Now... do I look all right?"

Excitement had shined her eyes and polished her cheeks. The filmy red cocktail dress was particularly becoming.

"You look great," Lindy assured her. "Steven will be so proud of you." It was the one compliment that could convince Celine.

She picked up her handbag. "I guess I'm ready then. Are you sure you want to watch the children, Lindy? You could still come with us. The babysitter's number is right by the phone."

"No, no . . . really. I'd rather stay with them. You and Steven have a wonderful time. Drink a little wine, take a walk in the moonlight . . ."

"Thanks, hon." Celine kissed her cheek. "Is your headache gone?"

"Just about."

"Good." Scribbling on a piece of paper, she added, "Here's where we'll be if you need us. Kids, come give Mommy a kiss."

They did, and with a wave Celine was gone in a cloud of chiffon. Lindy shut the door behind her, smiling fondly.

"Didn't your mom look pretty?"

"Yeah. Sure. Can we go to your room and play Parcheesi?"

They were in the middle of a hotly contested game when the phone rang.

"Hello?"

"Signorina Thorne?"

"Yes."

"One moment for Signor DiPalma."

Before she could reply, there was a crackling on the line and she heard his voice, sounding far away.

"Hello, Lindy?"

"Yes."

"Buona sera. Am I disturbing you?"

Not in any way he'd guess, she thought. "No, no. You sound like you're in Outer Mongolia."

His laughter was broken by static. "We just have a bad connection. . . . not at all unusual."

There was a pause, and Lindy tensed, fearful that he'd

mention Saturday night, their almost-kiss. If he apologized for it, she'd never forgive him.

"Listen...I was wondering..." A short silence ticked away, then his words came in a rush. "I just got a call from my office in Rome. They want me to attend a charity casino that's being given here tonight for some restoration cause. Lots of potential clients there. It's at a private *palazzo*, and I think you might enjoy seeing it. Would you like to come?...And of course, your sister and brother-in-law are most welcome."

When she didn't respond immediately, he added, "I know it's extremely rude of me to ask you at the last minute, but I've been...working hard these past two days, and the office just caught up with me. What do you say?"

"I'm sorry. I can't."

"I see." Did he sound disappointed? It was impossible to tell over the noisy wire.

"It's not that I wouldn't like to," she offered nonchalantly, "but Steven and Celine have gone out for the evening, and I'm staying with the children."

"Oh. . . . Listen, would your sister have any objections to a trustworthy substitute? I may be able to find a babysitter. . . ."

"Well, as a matter of fact"—Lindy drew a deep breath and plunged—"Celine used a sitter that the hotel recommended. I might be able to——"

"Benissimo! Check and call me right back, will you? Here's my number. . . ."

She jotted it down with a shaking hand. The line went dead, and she replaced the receiver slowly. She had to be crazy. How many times did she have to get burned?

Frowning, she crossed her arms stubbornly. He acted as if nothing had happened between them—nothing of consequence anyway. He'd probably dismissed it as a slight lapse in manners, rather like picking up the entrée fork for the salad—nothing terribly earthshaking, and easily forgotten. So why was *she* agonizing over it?

"I'm not that naive," she whispered fiercely. "I don't expect one kiss to lead to anything serious."

And she wasn't about to let him think she would wilt like a poor flower of a girl in a situation like this. She was nobody's drooping petunia... not any more.

"Hey, kids, remember Oriana? She sat with you the other day."

"Yeah. She was nice. And she played Parcheesi lots better than you."

"Oh, yeah? Well, if it's okay with your mom and dad, would you like her to stay with you tonight?"

"Oh, boy!"

"Yeah!"

Celine came to the phone out of breath, but only too ready to agree. "Of course, call her. And listen, if it's as ritzy as it sounds, you'd better dress up. You can wear my emerald earrings."

"Thanks just the same, Celine. I'll stick with my pearl ones."

"Okay, hon. Have a great time."

Oriana was happy to watch the twins. She promised to be there in fifteen minutes.

Lindy stared at the number she'd scrawled on the paper. Was it a hotel? Someone's home? How little she knew about Justin. Practically nothing.

He answered on the first ring. *"Pronto?"*

"I've spoken to Celine, and everything's arranged."

"Oh, good. The party's black-tie. May I pick you up at nine thirty?"

"That would be fine."

"See you then. *Ciao.*"

Hurrying through her preparations so she wouldn't have to think, Lindy then did everything twice to use up more time. She selected a dress from the wardrobe: high-necked, pale floral, romantic and maidenly. It went right back inside. In its place, she chose her white crepe. It wrapped around her body, hugging it sari-style, gathered to one shoulder and slit at the side.

She jumped when the telephone rang.

"Oriana, will you get that, please?"

Brush firmly in hand, Lindy flicked her hair to one side and drew it up on the other with a mother-of-pearl comb.

"Signor DiPalma is waiting."

"Thank you, Oriana."

Lingering a moment at the dressing table, Lindy let her hand hover over a crystal bottle. "Oh, what the hell," she muttered, dabbing the base of her throat with Shalimar perfume. "Might as well do it right."

Slipping on a white bias-cut cape, she studied herself in the mirror. This lady was no young innocent; she'd been to a few black-tie parties. She wouldn't pick up the wrong fork ever again.

He was waiting close to the elevator. When she caught sight of him, some of her determination faltered. His evening clothes fit him perfectly, emphasizing his muscular shoulders and narrow waist. He was so very good-looking, and she reacted so strongly to him, it was hard to remember her vow to show him how unconcerned she was.

She had a mad impulse to run, but his compelling eyes riveted her to the spot.

"You look . . . beautiful," he said softly.

Her lips parted in a bit of a smile, and it took a few seconds for her to find a polite but formal voice. "Thank you."

For a fraction of time, his forehead creased. Quickly smoothing it, he handed Lindy a square blue box. Curious, she opened it and spread the leaves of tissue paper.

It was a creamy white camellia. Gently, she touched the cool, waxy petals.

"It's just lovely. Thank you so much."

"May I?" Justin took the flower from her hand and pinned it to the shoulder of her gown. His fingers brushed her collarbone, seconds too long to be accidental. Her skin tingled where he touched her. She swallowed hard and avoided his eyes.

"Shall we go, Lindy?"

"Yes."

The motorboat ride to the *palazzo* on the Grand Canal was mercifully short. Neither of them spoke very much, which suited Lindy fine. But even in their silence, there was some intangible bond between them. It was a feeling of ... rightness. She couldn't define it, even to herself. And it troubled her.

"You may have heard of our hostess," Justin said as they stepped out of the boat. "She's an American heiress who has lived here for years. A lovely woman. Passionate about art and a strong supporter of preservation."

Passing through a wrought-iron gate, Lindy found herself in the most delightful courtyard, alive with the splash of fountains and the glow of tiny glass lanterns. They entered the palace. The foyer was larger than her whole apartment at home. Double doors to the left led to a huge ballroom with the most magnificent crystal chandelier she'd ever seen. A hundred exquisitely dressed people were gathered around gaming tables, and occasional refined murmurs indicated the winners.

The hostess was Mrs. Renniger, a beautiful woman in her mid-forties, who greeted them warmly and led them to an exchange booth. Wishing them good luck, she proceeded to other guests.

Justin peeled off what looked like half a sheaf of *lire* and was given a rack of markers in return. Seeing Lindy's expression, he laughed.

"Expense account. I'm not usually this carefree about throwing money around. Although I admit I enjoy games of chance. The excitement gets to me, the element of risk ... And you? Do you like to play?"

"Well, moderately. I told you I've become more cautious these days, remember?"

"Ah, yes. And do you remember me telling you that taking a chance can be ... most exhilarating?" He put his hand on her back to guide her just as a maid approached to take Lindy's wrap.

Lindy stepped out of his encircling arm and slipped

off her cape, well aware of the fleeting look of puzzle-
ment on Justin's smooth face. Let him think about it for
a while. Let him see that things like unconscious caresses
and near-kisses would not cause her to swoon.

They gravitated toward the roulette wheel, watching
the action until two seats became available. Justin placed
half his chips in front of Lindy, insisting when she de-
murred.

"You must help me spend this. Whatever we lose, it's
for a good cause."

She thought about it, pursing her lips. Then for the
next five or six spins, she put small bets on number
eleven, for her birthday. Justin's stacks were much taller,
and on different numbers every time. He seemed to have
caught her mood, and although he was unfailingly polite,
his conversation consisted mostly of comments on the
game.

More than once, Lindy intercepted speculative glances
from him. He chose his words carefully, and some of
the spontaneity between them was sacrificed. But, Lindy
reassured herself, there would be no disturbing surprises
this way.

"Signor DiPalma! So nice to see you."

"And you, Signora Molina. Has the flooding truly
subsided on the lower floor of your house?"

"Ah, si, si! Thanks to you."

"Bene. May I present..."

One after another, guests drifted to this, the largest
of the tables. As those he knew noticed him, they would
beam their hellos and introduce him to those he didn't
know. Lindy was secretly amazed that Justin mentioned
something special about each person he spoke to, even
the ones he'd just met. He obviously had done a vast
amount of homework.

"Ah, yes, *signor.* I hear you are having trouble with
the south wall of your building on Calle Mateo. Is the
ceiling also sagging?"

"Why, yes..."

"I'll drop around in the morning, if you like, to take a look. By the way, have you met Miss Melinda Thorne?"

Lindy knew that she was being appraised and that most of the reaction to her was favorable. She also knew that the same could be said of Justin—especially by the ladies.

Now don't start that again, she ordered herself. Remember, you're here to show him how perfectly blasé you can be.

In spite of her resolve to remain detached, the hypnotic spinning of the wheel and the satisfying click of the silver ball were beginning to relax her. On the next turn number eleven hit, and she couldn't suppress her jubilation.

The croupier was pushing her winnings toward her when she heard an ominously familiar voice.

"There you are, darling! I thought I might find you here tonight."

Before Justin could rise, Vittoria was upon him, taking advantage of his hemmed-in position and kissing him soundly on the cheek. With her back to Lindy, she scolded Justin playfully about avoiding her.

Lindy's face felt hot, and she tried to unclench her tightened jaw. Smiling stiffly at the croupier, she doubled her bet, ignoring the antics of the woman wedged between Justin and her.

"Oh, Giustino, I see your friend is here tonight too." The *contessa* finally acknowledged Lindy, flashing a smile that gave the lie to her cold black eyes. She wore huge topaz earrings and a clinging tangerine outfit that exposed much of her tawny flesh.

Outrageous dress, Lindy thought, nodding to Vittoria ever so slightly. Both color and cut. But she—damn it—had to look good in it.

"How are you, dear?" the *contessa* asked, not bothering to wait for a reply. "Giustino, doesn't she look sweet tonight, your Miss Thrump?"

"Thorne," Lindy said abruptly, but Vittoria had already turned away.

Lindy smacked a stack of chips down on number eleven, harder than she intended. The croupier looked up, and she laughed a little to cover her frustration.

"Signore e signori" —Mrs. Renniger's controlled voice floated through the ballroom—"Ladies and gentlemen."

The action stopped, and all attention went to a small platform where the hostess stood.

"Mille grazie, many thanks to all of you for being here tonight. I hope your luck hasn't been *all* good." There was a murmur of laughter. "I know you are all concerned about the preservation of this city—my adopted city—so I'd like to ask someone to speak to you, someone whose knowledge and tireless work is dedicated to maintaining the grandeur of Venice. . . . Signor Justin DiPalma!"

At the sound of encouraging applause, Justin rose. "Excuse me, please," he said, looking over the *contessa* at Lindy.

She watched him weave through the crowd, pausing now and then to grin and shake an outstretched hand. He was taller than most of the people there, and he moved as gracefully as a sleek Venetian cat. Mounting the platform, he kissed Mrs. Renniger's bejeweled hand, then faced the gathering.

"My friends. I too am glad to see all of you here. But unlike our gracious hostess, I hope your luck has been *terrible.*"

The assembly laughed in good humor. Somehow losing wasn't so bad, Lindy thought, when you were being complimented for it.

"We are all well aware," Justin was saying, more serious now, "of the challenges facing us. Nature and time are harsh masters, especially here in Venice, especially in an industrial age. But we must look at the positive side. The same technology that has caused problems can be used to solve those problems."

His gaze swept the silent room. Lindy watched him,

fascinated, unable to take her eyes from him. His expression was concentrated, intent. She could sense that coiled in his strong body was a barely controlled power. Why did she have this urge, this potent desire to see it unleashed?

"So, my friends, I'll give some advice for tonight only that you'll never hear from me again: Spend your money recklessly. *Venezia* is a demanding mistress!"

Justin was caught in the enthusiastic applause. As he slowly worked his way back to the roulette table, Vittoria edged into his chair beside Lindy.

"Ah," she sighed, eyes heavenward, "these Italian men. They seduce a woman with beautiful words, even before they touch her. Hard to resist, no? But with some of them—some special men—one has no means to resist." Vittoria sighed again, but her gaze was calculating. "Don't you agree, Miss Thrump?"

"The name is Thorne," Lindy said coolly. "As in what pricks your finger when you get too close to a rose. And no, *contessa,* I don't agree. One can always resist, if she has the inclination."

Vittoria's eyebrow lifted haughtily, but she said nothing.

Arriving at the table, Justin immediately sized up the situation. "Lindy, do you mind? I have a very early appointment tomorrow...."

"I understand," she replied, pointedly snubbing Vittoria. "Shall we go?"

"Your winnings, *signorina,*" the croupier indicated a pile of chips he feared Lindy would forget to take.

"Would you please give them to Mrs. Renniger, with my compliments?"

"*Certamente, signorina.*"

Justin pushed his rack of chips to the side. "Mine too, please."

"*Si, signor.*"

He retrieved her cape and placed it on her shoulders, this time without touching her. "That was a lovely gesture, giving your markers to Gladys."

Lindy smiled, calming down. "Your speech was very inspiring."

They passed through the foyer and into the charming courtyard. The night breeze licked at the lantern lights.

"Sometimes," Justin said softly, "I can get carried away with...enthusiasm, or something, for the things that matter deeply to me. I'm afraid that tends to scare some people off."

"Well," Lindy said dryly, "maybe *some* people. Others seem to be wildly attracted to it."

He glanced sideways at her. "You mean the *contessa*. Ah, yes, she keeps insisting that I talk her out of her plans for the Palazzo D'Alente. Frankly, I don't think she quite knows *what* she wants to do with it."

Maybe not, Lindy thought grimly, but there was no doubt about what else the *contessa* wanted—Justin himself.

There was no waiting for the boat this time. The pilot, a man younger and less cheerful than Giacomo, had the engine revved up before they boarded.

As they rode without speaking, skimming the black waters of the canal, Lindy found her temper rising once more. Vittoria was unbelievably pushy about wanting Justin, but it was nothing new to Lindy. How many times had she seen women like that, poised to pounce on Blair? Different faces and names, but the same species, the same relentless stalking. They abided by the law of the jungle, the survival of the fittest. Oh, yes, she felt she knew the Contessa D'Alente extremely well.

And now that she recognized her for what she was, somehow Lindy didn't feel quite so threatened by her. Since she'd decided not to become involved with Justin, what did it matter anyway? He was certainly capable of fending off Vittoria, if he wanted to....

If he wanted to.

Drawing her cape closer, Lindy squared her shoulders. The motorboat slowed beside the quay, and when Justin

helped her out, his touch was light, courteous but un-
demanding. Just the way she wanted it, right?

"Thank you for going with me on such short notice,"
he murmured, walking her to the lobby of the Royal
Danieli. Inside the door, he stopped and gazed down at
her.

"I enjoyed this evening," he said, but there was an
uncertainty in his beautiful moss-green eyes, a mild question he didn't want to ask.

"Thank you," Lindy replied, her voice faltering
slightly. "I enjoyed it too."

He pressed her hand to his lips, then rubbed her fingers
gently between his for a moment. "I'll call you. . . ."

"Yes . . . *Buona notte.*"

"*Buona notte.*" He smiled, swiftly searching her face
before he turned and walked into the night.

Well, she'd done it, Lindy thought, ignoring the hollow, incomplete feeling she had inside. She'd showed
him she could stay uninvolved. Just friends. Nothing
complicated.

It wasn't until she was in her room, until she removed
the camellia and stroked the browning petals across her
cheek, that the tears began welling in her eyes.

Lindy spent a restless night, awakened again and again
by a vague sadness, never quite identifying it, drifting
back into wisps of sleep. It was nearly eleven the next
morning before she could drag herself out of bed, feeling
achy and exhausted.

Celine had slipped a note under her door, saying that
she'd taken the twins to the Napoleon Gardens to work
off steam. Lindy should join them for a picnic lunch.

For a moment she considered it: Napoleon
Gardens . . . trees and grass, rare commodities in Venice
. . . perhaps an antidote to the illusory light of the city,
enabling her to clear her fuzzy head and think straight.
That part sounded good. Todd and Tammy cavorting like
little wood nymphs; Celine asking nonstop questions that

had no answers. That part sounded not so good.

Glancing into the rococo mirror, she almost had to laugh. She'd seen better-looking hangovers.

"Perk up, kid," she murmured to the bleary-eyed image. "You'll most likely survive."

Napoleon Gardens? No, not today. But there was a small park, just beyond St. Mark's, the Giardinetti Reali. It might provide the clarifying bit of greenery she needed.

Yanking on a candy-striped dress, grabbing her straw purse and dark glasses and a wide-brimmed raffia hat she'd bought in the market, Lindy hurried outside.

The sunshine immediately enveloped her, slowing her steps. An intermittent breeze blew in from the Adriatic, urging her to breathe deeply of the scent of the sea. To her great surprise, Lindy found herself looking up with pleasure as she passed the colonnades of the Doges' Palace. By the time she'd gone by San Marco and the arcade of the Procuratie Nuove, she was nearly smiling.

The little royal gardens—Giardinetti Reali—were cool and peaceful at this hour, when only the crazy *turisti* ventured out of doors. She found a shaded bench that overlooked the Basin of St. Mark. The water rippled with activity from chunky work boats and sleek power skiffs. Leaning back, Lindy gazed upward at the trees, their leaves ruffled by the wind.

The effect was calming, but the whispering trees offered no answers either. She simply did not understand what was going on with her. After refusing to become entangled with Justin, having steadfastly maintained her distance last night, she should be happy, or at least proud of herself. With a sigh, she admitted that she was neither.

An inquiring meow drew her attention to the sidewalk. A black-and-white cat waited patiently to see if Lindy would offer a morsel of fish or cheese.

"Sorry, fella," she murmured. "I don't have a thing to share with you." The feline sat a moment, focusing his unblinking jade gaze on her.

"Oh, those beautiful green eyes," she whispered. The

cat, sensing that she spoke of another, arched his back and padded away.

Her firm resolve was fine, if only it didn't melt like hot butter when Justin was around. She could tick off a dozen good reasons for following the course she'd chosen with him, but they'd sift right through her fingers when he accidentally brushed against her. She could make all the rules she liked, but they didn't mean a thing as long as her instinctive response to him was so powerful.

"I just have to stop seeing him," she decided aloud, testing the thought, seeing what impact it had on that still-hollow core of herself.

None. She felt no different.

It was better like that. Justin probably was not the best man to fall for anyway. The only thing that really captivated him was his work, preserving antiquity, shoring up crumbling palaces . . . such as the Palazzo D'Alente.

At the thought of Vittoria, Lindy's stomach tightened. That woman undoubtedly did not set limits for herself. She'd go after Justin with talons extended. And no man resisted very long in the face of such dazzling determination.

Crossing her arms over her middle, Lindy looked glumly out to the water. Determined . . . yes, the eager *contessa* certainly was that, and single-minded where Justin was concerned.

Frowning, Lindy rolled that thought around in her head. Vittoria was almost *too* single-minded. Women who radiated so much sensuality never worked that hard on one man. They didn't have to. There were always half a dozen more waiting in the wings, one more handsome, more charming, more wealthy than the next.

And that was another thing: For Vittoria's ilk, dashing young architects were exciting playmates, diverting lovers. But one first established a solid base, usually a well-heeled older man who provided the respectability of marriage and the security of diamonds and trust funds.

The *contessa* had her priorities confused; and she was much too shrewd to do that unwittingly.

"So what is she up to?" Lindy muttered.

All the Byzantine intrigue surrounding the *contessa* was too intricate for Lindy's straightforward American mind. She was no match for these Venetians.

Including Justin?

She closed her eyes, sighing. It was getting more complicated by the moment. Slowly, thoughtfully, she strolled back to the hotel, more confused than ever.

- 7 -

"HELLO?"

"Hello, Lindy. How are you?"

Her grip tightened on the telephone and she inhaled sharply.

"I...I'm fine, Justin. And you?"

"Very well."

In the silence that followed, Lindy tried to think of something to say. Her mind seemed studded with blank spaces.

"Listen," he began hesitantly. "I want to apologize for not calling sooner. I had to go to Rome on Tuesday."

Three days ago...no call, no message. Well, what had she expected?

"That's all right. Actually, I've been quite busy. I mean, I probably wouldn't have been here if you *had* tried to call." She bit her lip. Stupid.

"As a matter of fact, I did—try, that is—but the telephone workers were on strike, and I couldn't get through. Not," he added hastily, "that that's any excuse."

But it was, and Lindy felt a small part of herself thawing.

"So how was your trip?"

"Good." Even over the wire his laugh was full-bodied. "Well, successful, anyway. I spent my time altering a restoration plan and refereeing an argument between two designers. Just being my indispensible self."

There was a touch of irony in his voice that reminded Lindy of the Justin she'd seen in the Rialto markets. Had they gone there only a week ago? It seemed he'd been on her mind for months.

He cleared his throat. "Listen, I wanted to tell you . . . I understand perfectly if you want to call off our sailing date. I know you must think I'm terribly rude——"

"No, no," she cut in quickly. "Uh, what I mean is, to tell you the truth"—for the hundredth time that week, she glanced at the glass sailboat he'd given her. The morning sunlight shot its cobalt and turquoise with life— "I nearly forgot about the whole thing."

"Oh. Well, I understand. You did say you've been busy. . . ." He sounded almost resigned. "I have to tell you one more thing. I truly enjoyed the time we had together. I . . . I usually don't take much time off. There are so many details to attend to in my work. . . . And frankly, I find most social occasions very dull and pointless. But when we were together . . ." His voice trailed off. When he spoke again, it was tender, almost a murmur. "I found it a great pleasure."

She let his words tumble around in her head, unaware of the secret smile that played on her lips. A great pleasure . . . yes, yes indeed. The memory lulled her, so that she heard not so much what he said next, but what his words implied.

". . . ask that you always remember the fine times we had and not my discourtesy."

There was a finality in his words, a few swift strokes to close the circle. But that was what she wanted, wasn't it? To end whatever was between them now, before it spiraled into something too big to ignore? Wasn't that her plan?

"Arrive——"

"Wait!" she gasped, realizing a sliver of panic. "I certainly can't hold you responsible for a strike in Rome." Her laugh came in a nervous squeak, but she didn't care. "And if you must know, my feet feel as though I've walked a hundred miles since I've been here. So a sail would be heavenly."

"It would?"

"Yes, it would."

"When?" His mood seemed suddenly buoyant; he sounded eager.

"Whenever you like."

"The weather for today is supposed to be nearly perfect—only a few high clouds and a decent breeze . . . What do you say?"

"I can be ready in half an hour."

Lindy was fully aware, as she replaced the receiver with a whoop, of the import of the last sixty seconds. She knew that in one tick of the clock she had stripped away the armor she'd needed painstaking hours to fashion. She gave the realization a fleeting thought as she rummaged for a terry-cloth tank top and her swimsuit, wondering if she should feel guilty—or doomed. Just as rapidly, she dismissed it. The only thing she felt was infinitely lighter.

This time she was waiting for him in the lobby. A buttoned salmon-colored skirt covering her suit, she sat on the edge of an antique love seat, unashamedly watching the doorway. When an overdressed matron sniffed at Lindy's bare shoulders and espadrilles, she promptly opened another button on the skirt, exposing three inches of tanned skin above her knee. Her rigid rules had been discarded with the armor.

She was on her feet as soon as Justin strode through the door. He had an innately captivating presence. Eyes followed him, even now, in his casual jeans and white polo shirt. He looked neither left nor right, but straight at her. The glow of his smile warmed her from across the lobby.

She met him halfway.

"Hi."

"Hello."

Somehow, without her knowing it, their hands had met. He squeezed hers lightly, and she returned the gesture, pulled almost on tiptoe by the vitality zinging through her.

"I've got a sweet little sloop reserved on the Lido," he said, his eyes gleaming. "Ready?"

"Uh-huh."

Lindy's face was lit by a smile that would not dim. He rushed her out to the dock, to a skiff with motor running and Giacomo standing itchily at the helm. The boat began cutting through the choppy water, and they settled into the rear seat, their bodies touching in the fluid el of arm and thigh.

Leaning back, Lindy tipped her face to the climbing sun, absorbing its blessing. She felt no urge to speak. The droning motor filled the silence quite comfortably.

Giacomo, unfettered by twisting canals, made a full-throttled beeline for the Lido shore. Every so often, as they sped past one of the many little islands dotting the lagoon, he would point and bark a name over his shoulder.

"San Servolo!"

"Sant'Elena!"

"Porto di Lido!"

Lindy looked up with interest. They were rounding the narrow sandbar of the Lido and heading into the Adriatic Sea. It spread before them, wide and smooth. She shaded her eyes against the sun-scattered diamonds on the water.

"Nice?"

Glancing up at Justin, she smiled her appreciation. Unexpectedly, he laced his fingers through hers.

"You know, Lindy... I've missed you."

She blinked, and he nodded, confirming his words.

Before she could reply, he called to Giacomo and gestured at a point on the beach. They shot toward a rocky pier at top speed, and just as Lindy was sure they'd crash into it, Giacomo killed the engine. Almost immediately, the craft slowed, its wake backwashing and sending it in a surge to the wooden boat-landing. It stopped a miraculous three inches from the pilings.

Lindy let out a sigh of relief, and Justin chuckled.

"Takes some getting used to, doesn't it?"

"I doubt that I ever will."

The rented blue-and-white sailboat was waiting for them, snuggled into its slip, the mast swaying drowsily in the breeze. The attendant, mahogany-skinned, wearing the merest hint of a swimsuit, ushered them aboard. Opening a small forward cabin, he showed them extra line, towels, and surprisingly, a large wicker picnic basket. With a wave and a *ciao,* he was gone.

Justin dunked the tail of the tiny outboard motor into the water and pulled the starter. It gave an angry hum. Without having to be told, Lindy manned the forward line, stepping out of the awkward skirt and tossing it into the cockpit.

"Okay!" Justin nodded, and she threw off the moorings.

Lindy stayed on the bow as the sloop nudged out of the little harbor. The wind kicked at her curls, and she smiled, taking a deep, satisfying breath.

"Do you want to take the helm," Justin called, "while I raise the jib?"

"I can get it," she answered, already peeling off the canvas cover. With the ease of practice, she hoisted the sail and it went singing up the mast. The wind caught, and the sail bulged white against the bright azure sky.

"Perfect," Justin declared, as she hopped back into the cockpit. "You really do know your way around a boat, don't you?"

She hated to admit how much his admiration cheered her. While she was busy forward, he'd zipped out of his jeans to a pair of white trunks. He sat on one of the molded side-seats, his hand resting lightly on the secured tiller, his tanned, muscular legs propped casually on the seat across. Lindy settled down opposite him, stretching her feet out when he patted the bench beside him.

They glided quietly on the sea for a while, until the shouts of the swimmers at the beach were swallowed up by distance and they heard only the splash of the bow and an occasional screeching gull.

"Isn't this the ideal antidote to sightseeing?"

Chuckling, Lindy wiggled out of her shoes. "It certainly is. And I haven't had many chances to be out on the water this summer."

"Where did you learn to sail?"

"I grew up by Lake George, in New York. My father taught me." Her face softened, remembering. "He was a merchant seaman, grounded by a sickly wife and two daughters. He said that if he couldn't be on the sea, he didn't want to sit around looking at it. So, after one last, long cruise, he gave up his card and bought a little boat-repair business on the lake. Every spare minute, he was out on the water."

"And you went with him?"

Lindy laughed. "It was the only way to have him to myself. And eventually, without even meaning to, I learned how to sail. It kind of grew on me. Pretty soon, I began to miss it if I didn't go out every day in the summer."

Justin scanned the horizon contentedly. "It's the peace. No one is tugging at your sleeve or nipping at your heels out here. You can think . . . put things in perspective. When you and your boat are the only objects between ocean and sky, you realize the significance of things. What's really important and what's just—" Breaking off, he smiled, slightly sheepish. "I didn't mean to go all philosophical on you. It's been a long time for me, too. I'd forgotten *how* long. I've been so busy with the nippers and the tuggers."

Lindy nodded, understanding only too well. She felt

a sort of kinship with him, and she sensed it went deeper than their mutual love of the water.

"I did some of my best thinking in a boat. That was another thing Dad taught me. It was sort of like running away from home without really meaning it."

"The way you talk about your father..." Justin hesitated, probing gently. "It's always in the past tense."

"Yes...he died when I was fourteen." It was a dull, vaguely remembered ache by now. Still, her eyes misted for a second. "I think...I think he withered away because he had no more dreams."

Startled by her own voice, she glanced at Justin and shrugged to hide her confusion. That thought about her father had always dwelt secretly in her mind. She'd never before let it out, not with her mother, not with Celine.

"So where did you learn to sail?" she asked, to change the subject.

"In the Bay area...San Francisco, where I grew up. And at Lago di Como, in the Italian Alps. I spent my summers there with *Nonno*."

"Who?"

"*Nonno*—my grandfather." He smiled, thinking about it. "He was a tough old bird. And he expected me to be just as hardy as he was. He thought life in America had softened me up. So every day I had to take a swim in the lake. Have you ever been to Lake Como?"

"No," she admitted.

"It's fed by mountain streams and springs. Freezing cold, even in August. To this day I can feel that first plunge...like a million needles going through me." Justin gave a mock shiver and laughed in his clear baritone. "But you know something? I did it. Every blessed day I was there. And do you know why? Because that barrel-chested, opinionated, seventy-year-old man was right alongside me, matching me stroke for stroke."

He shook his head with affection. "Some guy. You should have seen him. He was tall, with pure white hair and the fiercest scowl....I used to think *Nonno* was like a mountain himself, snow-covered and hard as a rock."

Almost absently, he checked the compass and adjusted the tiller a degree or so. He seemed so much more relaxed on the water, Lindy noticed.

"We lived in an old chalet." When he caught Lindy's impressed nod, he grinned. "Wait, it's not what you think. It had belonged to generations of goatherds, very small, built into the hillside. The ground floor had been the stable, but *Nonno* kept his tools and wine there. Actually, that was my first work on a restoration. We replaced missing stones in the walls and fireplace. It was really exciting to me, thinking that the cabin we saw was basically the same one the goatherds had lived in for two or three hundred years...."

Pausing, he gazed at Lindy speculatively, and after a moment, she knew why. They had each peeled away a layer of their social selves, something Lindy realized was as rare a concession for her as for him. She hadn't known how tightly she'd insulated herself, but it was a marvelous feeling to shed even one band of it. And curiously, Justin appeared to be experiencing it too.

"You know, Lindy, I haven't thought about *Nonno* for a very long time. There always seem to be a thousand things vying for my attention.... But he's one person I should think about a lot. He's the reason I do what I do. Not only because of the cabin, but also because of his theory of save-a-place."

It was Lindy's turn to smile, her brow wrinkling slightly.

"What?"

"Oh, *Nonno* believed that history saved a place for every living soul and that you couldn't possibly know where you fit in unless you knew where your grandparents and great-grandparents and great-great... Well, you get the idea. So every summer, while we were fixing up the cabin, he'd give me a running commentary, an oral history of the DiPalma family for eons back. He knew a boy didn't learn these things in San Francisco. It was one item in a yard-long list of grievances he had about

America in general, and my father in particular. People dropped their ancestors in the 'melt pot,' as he liked to call it, when they passed Ellis Island."

Justin exchanged a smile with Lindy, then shook his head.

"Crazy old bird. He died the summer I was sixteen, right after we'd finally finished the chalet. It was as though his work was done and he was moving on. I guess that's when I decided to become an architect."

It was a large piece of himself that he'd given, and Lindy appreciated it. She found herself wishing she'd known him then, when his limbs were long and coltish and his eyes as tender as spring mountain grass.

"So how," she asked, "did you come to live in Italy?"

"I took a graduation trip to Rome after I got my degree. See, *Nonno* had never taken me any further than Florence. He claimed the water was unfit to bathe in, much less drink, in the south. So there I was in Rome, with all this save-a-place history surrounding me. I was like a kid in a candy store. I spent one whole day just wandering around the Roman Forum. Such weird sensations... it made me half-mad that no one had been around in the first century to preserve this for me in the twentieth. I happened to mention that to the cab driver on the way back to my hotel. And boy, did that set him off! He started waving his hands and screaming that I must be insane, I must be one of those *Bell 'Italia* jackasses. Traffic was bad enough; did I want to block off streets so some stupid statue wouldn't fall down?"

"So you..." Lindy prompted.

"So I decided this *Bell 'Italia* sounded pretty good, and I looked into it. Within the month, I had signed on."

The bow dipped into a small swell, spraying their laughter with salt water. Justin's hand dropped down to the bench, accidentally brushing Lindy's bare foot. Still smiling, he rubbed her arch with his strong thumb. She froze as her senses leaped to life. A few seconds crept by where there was no other movement from either of them. Finally it was Justin who broke the spell.

"I have to come around to starboard. Watch your head."

Lindy ducked so that her brow was nearly touching her knees. Justin moved the tiller, and the boom swung over her with a metallic creak. Straightening up and squinting at the horizon, Lindy detected a hazy gray green form.

"Is that where we're heading?" she asked, pointing.

Following her gaze, he nodded. "A little island— uninhabited now. Good place for a picnic."

"How'd you ever find it?"

"Believe it or not, there's an old ruin on it. Not enough remains to tell for sure, but I think it was a pirates' lair once. There are some deceptive shallows on the windward side—probably caused quite a few shipwrecks long ago. Nothing but the stone foundation is left now."

"You'd make some detective," Lindy said.

"I would?" His eyes twinkled like the sun on the sea. "What makes you think so and how do you know?"

"What makes me think so," she retorted genially, "is that you are a digger. You search for reasons beyond the facts on the surface. How I know is that I'm like that too."

"Oh. Nosy, you mean."

"No, not nosy. Sort of . . . perversely curious."

"Oh, great. Sounds like we could get arrested for that."

She made a face at him, and when he grinned, she had to join him.

"Come on, now, think about it. For instance, when that cabbie said all those terrible things about *Bell'Italia,* what did you do? You beat a path to their door to find out who and what they were. Instead of shying away from controversy, you plunge right into it with both feet, now don't you?"

He held up his palms to her. "I confess. Now *you* tell me—do you do that too?"

Tilting her head back, she sighed. "I used to. In fact, I got paid to. I had a radio talk show in upstate New

York, not too far from where I grew up. Guests would come on, I'd interview them, then the listeners could call in with questions or comments."

"Sounds fascinating."

"It was. Until I plunged a little too deep. Remember those needles you felt in Lake Como? I got that too, right after my most infamous dive into controversy. Only, in my case, the needles came from my boss's eyes."

- *8* -

THE GOLD IN Justin's eyes flickered with interest, and she thought back to that difficult period when she'd started rebuilding her life after her divorce, now almost two years ago. She'd told Blair to keep their East Sixties townhouse, wanting nothing more than to slink out of New York City and lick her wounds in a quiet place where Blair Talbot's name wouldn't mock her from gossip columns. Celine kept urging her toward some old friends.

"You remember Laura Schick?" she'd asked Lindy one day. "She and Ed moved upstate and bought a little radio station. I . . . er . . . just happened to talk to her the other day, and what do you know? Ed's assistant producer for the nighttime phone-in talk show up and quit. You could be a big help to him, Lindy. You know— doing research and lining up guests and things like that. You'd be real good at it."

And she was. So good, in fact, that when the host suddenly broke contract to move on to bigger and better things in another part of the country, Ed Schick had turned to her.

"Lindy, Bob's pulled a fast one in his march to the big time, and it seems we're stuck for tonight's broadcast. You're going on for him...in fifteen minutes."

"But...but I've never—" she'd protested. "I don't have any experience...."

"You've read commercials on the air, haven't you? And you did all the research on tonight's guest. It shouldn't be much of a problem for you."

And surprisingly to Lindy, it wasn't. After her initial nervousness faded, she actually began to enjoy herself. That evening's guest had written a thoughtful book on parent-teen-ager communication, and spoke easily and well. Listener response to the phone-in discussion was enthusiastic. Within two weeks, she was no longer "Melinda Thorne, substituting for Bob Maxwell," but the official host.

As the year quickly passed, Ed Schick let her select more and more of her own guests. She found herself seeking out the unusual, the controversial. Phone-ins were always heaviest with such topics, and Lindy craved the excitement that the heated discussions provoked in her—mostly because it was the only stimulation she allowed herself. Her life was a sphere bounded by her oak-and-chintz apartment and occasional visits with Ed and Laura. The center of the sphere was her work.

Her whole day focused on the hours between 11 P.M. and 1 A.M. Secretly, she marveled at her luck in finding what seemed to her the perfect position. She loved meeting the odd people, from geniuses to flakes; she enjoyed the contradiction of being a famous voice and an unknown face; and though she didn't care to admit it to Laura or especially to Celine, she was relieved to have the excuse of constant deadline pressure to turn aside their careful approaches to matchmaking. But best of all, the lonely void of the evening was filled. She didn't have to wonder and wish...and remember how much Blair had hurt her.

Then that whole life was cruelly dissolved in about fifteen seconds of air time.

It had begun with a subject tailor-made for "Let's Talk." A local woman, much abused mentally and physically by her husband, had in desperation shot him. He recovered, only to press charges of attempted murder against her. He hooked up with an ambitious assistant prosecutor, and together they dragged her reputation through the mud. The Claire Conway case was angrily argued all over town, and nowhere as fervidly as on Lindy's show.

Ed was ecstatic.

"Lindy, if this dame can hang on for one more week, we can sell another huge block of advertising for your show. There might even be a bonus in it for you, my girl."

She pressed her lips together, saying nothing.

"What's the matter with you? This is the biggest break we ever had for 'Let's Talk.' We got more calls, more letters——"

"Ed, Claire Conway's life, her whole future, is at stake here. She took that man's beatings, his malicious verbal attacks . . . he practically killed her on more than one occasion. And when she finally strikes back, he accuses *her* of a crime and gets away with it! It's a damn shame, that's what it is. How can you get so excited over the profit in it? And don't 'my girl' me!"

Ed said no more about the matter, and Lindy concentrated as always on new material, new guests. Until the day the verdict was returned: guilty as charged. Mrs. Conway was sentenced to ten years in prison, and Ed booked the assistant prosecutor and hired the city auditorium to do the show live, in front of an audience, in prime time.

"You what?"

"Now, now, Lindy, take it easy. This is business. You're a professional; you can handle it. Our switchboard will light up like Times Square on New Year's Eve."

The appeal to her pride in her work sealed it. Advance publicity spots were broadcast ten times a day, and the show opened with the biggest fanfare in the station's history.

She almost made it. There were only nine minutes left when Ranston, the deputy prosecutor, announced smugly that he was sure justice had been served. Lindy's tightly coiled anger snapped.

"Listen, buster. The only thing that has been 'served' in this case is a bunch of baloney—to Claire Conway and to any woman who suffers the way she did. As far as I'm concerned, you *and* Judge Dixon ought to be shot for helping Conway get away with it. And furthermore, I'll be damned if I'll sit on the same stage with you for another minute."

With that, Lindy stomped out of the hall, out of the building, and home. Ed's prediction came true; the switchboard nearly blew a fuse, but that was nothing compared to the shock wave that swept the crowd in the auditorium.

When Ed marched into her apartment two hours later, Lindy was stretched out on the sofa, a large brandy and soda in her hand.

"What in the *hell* did you think you were doing?"

She glanced sheepishly at his scarlet complexion for a second, then frowned and set her chin in a stubborn line. "That guy was a jerk from the word *go*. He wasn't even a good guest. Every time I'd ask him a question, he'd slide all around the answer." Lindy shuddered. "Ooh, what a creep! No wonder——"

"Do you know what I've been doing for the last two hours?" Schick's calm was forced; the veins in his thick neck throbbed. "I've been on the phone getting my attorneys out of bed, because after you left, Ranston didn't slide around anything. He came right to the point. We can expect a lawsuit that will make the Conway case look like a kindergarten quarrel."

She couldn't stop herself. "Think of the advertising *that* will sell."

Ed's round face purpled, and she immediately lifted a peacemaking hand. "I was only kidding."

"Some joke."

"Come on, Ed, sit down. I'll fix you a drink."

When he had gulped down the contents of the glass, his color faded to normal. He blew a heavy sigh past his jowls.

"You know, I've been doing 'Let's Talk' for four years now. In all that time, I've only had to use the ten-second delay maybe two, three times a week. Usually because some caller let a cuss word slip or some kid's playing tricks with the phone. The one time we do a live remote, and you knife me in the back."

Lindy rubbed at the beginnings of a headache.

"Look, isn't that why we have a disclaimer at the start of the show? You know: 'The opinions expressed by Melinda Thorne are her own and do not...' etcetera, etcetera."

"Yeah, well, that's our only chance," Ed conceded, emptying his glass down his throat. "Most people realize that you didn't mean those two guys should be shot *literally*." He glanced at her with suspicion. "It *was* just a figure of speech, wasn't it?"

Lindy's smile was beatific.

"Well, tomorrow when we go on the air, you'll apologize. And from now on, we stick to do-it-yourself books and *Making Friends With Your Subconscious*. No more of this powder keg stuff."

The apology she could have handled—she was chagrined at her own breach of professionalism, although her opinion of Ranston held firm—but to remove the excitement from her show? Ed might as well drain her blood.

"Ed, I can't do it!"

"You don't have a choice. I can't afford it any other way."

"But I can't do the show like that! It just won't work."

"Well... so be it."

Lindy holed up in her apartment and cried for three

days, ignoring the telephone and the doorbell. Finally, she opened the door a crack to Laura.

"At least call your sister, Lindy. She's been worried sick about you."

"How did she know?"

"Uh . . . well, I just happened to talk to her the other day. Really . . . call her. Just tell her you're all right. You *are* all right, aren't you?"

"Yeah . . . yeah. Okay, I'll give her a ring."

Celine's relief flooded through the wire.

"Oh, this is just the most perfect timing. Steven has to go to Italy next month—to Venice!—on business, and the twins and I are going along. Now you can come too."

"Oh, Celine, I don't know . . ."

"If it's the money, don't even think about it. They've booked us a suite at the most elegant hotel in the whole city, and I'm sure we'll be wined and dined every night." She paused a second, sensing her sister's wavering. "Oh, come on, Lindy. I need somebody to see the sights with while Steven's at his meetings. Better you than some romantic Italian, no?"

The memory of Celine's words brought Lindy quickly back into the present with a start, and a smile. Here *she* was with the romantic Italian, while her sister was seeing the sights with her two ten-year-olds. She looked up at Justin, at his warm gold-green eyes full of expectation and understanding, and for the first time she had the desire to tell someone about her experience at the station. Briefly, she recounted the tale of Claire Conway and her own outburst on the air. Contemplating for a second, she then shrugged.

"Ed was a good man. But after that, he wanted me to do the lukewarm stuff, and I simply couldn't."

"I can understand that."

She glanced over at him. "You can?"

"Sure. I saw it in you from the beginning." The wind rippled his silky black hair. It didn't touch his steady gaze. "We even spoke about it, remember? The spice of risk?"

"Yes," she said softly, unable—unwilling—to break the contact of their eyes. "And I told you it got me in trouble. I'm not so ready to jump in headfirst these days. I like to test the water very carefully before I even consider it."

A sudden shift in the wind distracted her, and she busied herself adjusting the sail, grateful for the diversion. She was finding it too temptingly easy to get lost in the way he looked at her.

"Tell me, Lindy," Justin said as she reclaimed her seat on the bench. "What do you plan to do when you go home?"

She considered it a moment.

"I hadn't really thought about it. . . . Probably try to find another radio job. Maybe behind the scenes this time. Nothing big. Just enough to support myself and justify my turning down alimony."

"You were married?" His eyebrows raised a fraction.

She hadn't meant to tell him, it had just slipped out.

"Yes, once. It was a mistake from the start. We were too opposite, and very young. Fortunately, I . . . we realized it before it dragged on for too long." Venturing a glance at him, she added, "You seem surprised."

He lifted his hand from the tiller, then let it fall back again.

"No, no. I was just wondering . . ."

"What?"

"Oh . . . nothing." He took a quick survey of the approaching shoreline. "The wind's picking up. Do you want to look out for shoals?"

Lindy moved forward, shading her eyes and searching for the sea's caution signs: jagged little waves that indicated rocks, light-colored pools that disguised shallow water.

"Ten degrees to port," she warned once through the wind whistling in the rigging. That was all the oral communication they needed.

More details of the island emerged as they got closer.
It appeared to be overwhelmed by lush greenery, except
for a sandy crescent of beach.

"Get ready to lower the jib," Justin called. "We'll
have to anchor out."

She responded immediately to his "Now!" and he
dropped the anchor. When the sail was secured, she
jumped back into the cockpit.

"Does this mean we swim ashore?"

"Not unless you want to. Look." Reaching in the
forward locker, he pulled out an inflatable raft. He held
onto its line and tossed it overboard, yanking the rope
as he did. With a hiss, it popped open and filled with
air, bobbing proudly.

"Great!" Lindy laughed.

Justin crawled in kneeling, and she passed him the
wicker basket and a pile of towels. As she stepped
aboard, he put his hands on her waist, steadying her. She
was shocked at the impact of his gentle grip, his fingers
pressing into her back.

There was only one paddle, and he took it, dipping
it in and out of the water with sure, swift strokes. As
soon as the raft scraped bottom, they both hopped out
and tugged it ashore.

Lindy looked around happily. The pristine sand reflected the sun's warmth. Here and there graceful strings
of seaweed dried themselves in the early afternoon air.
A bare twenty yards away, the foliage was creeping toward the Adriatic.

She couldn't restrain her delight. "Oh, this is beautiful!"

"Isn't it?" Justin agreed, sharing her appreciation.
"What'll we do first, have a swim or eat lunch?"

"Oh, lunch definitely. The sea air always leaves me
famished."

He sighed dramatically. "I'm so glad you said that.
Let's eat!"

They spread the aquamarine towels and sat cross-
legged on either side of the basket, taking turns pulling

out the contents. There was a stick of salami, and three kinds of cheese, and little plastic containers of olives and sweet peppers. An insulated pouch held a lightly chilled bottle of Bardolino. A checkered cloth wrapped a crusty loaf of Italian bread.

"Utopia!" Lindy declared, breaking off a hunk and offering it to Justin. "This is really terrific. I'm glad I came."

Trading her a few slices of meat, he shook his head. "To tell you the truth, I didn't think you would."

"Really? Why not?"

"Well . . ." He hesitated, measuring her for a moment. After a rapid decision, he continued, ". . . the last time we were together, at Mrs. Renniger's, I thought you were annoyed with me. And rightfully so, I must add. I know I was truly presumptuous, asking you at the last minute. And I did it today too. It's just that—"

He seemed uneasy in his search for the right words, irritated and puzzled when they eluded him. Squirming, Lindy reminded herself that his lapse of manners wasn't even remotely connected to her annoyance that night.

"Justin, it's all right. You don't have to——"

"No. It's very important to me that you understand. You see, I'm somewhat of a lone wolf, I'm most comfortable by myself. It's a strange sensation, wanting to be with another person. And that's the situation I found myself in this week. I wanted to be with you."

There was a tinge, a very slight but detectable tinge, of wonder in his voice. She felt it racing through her bloodstream.

"You did?"

"Yes."

For a brief space of time, they seemed to be at a brink, but Lindy's thoughts were swirling too much to be able to identify it. Finally, it was Justin who backed off.

"Well, anyway, I'm glad you came too."

He poured two tumblers of wine and gave a jaunty salute. "To picnics."

Lindy fairly gulped the cool Bardolino.

"You know, my little friend, you would make my Italian colleagues very pleased."

"I'm thirsty," she said in defense, blushing.

Justin laughed heartily.

"No, no. I mean the fact that you got me to take a whole day off. I drive them crazy. I think it all stems from the fact that, try as I might, I cannot get used to the siesta, the waste of two valuable hours in the middle of the day, especially in an air-conditioned office, where the heat is immaterial. That's the American in me. There's a streak of the Puritan in all of us."

He glanced at Lindy to see if he'd lightened her mood. She smiled to let him know he had.

"But if I spend too many days like today"—his look encompassed sea and sky and island—"I could come to appreciate it. And that's my Italian coming out at last."

It was that duality that Lindy had sensed in him from the first.

"It must be strange," she began slowly, pondering it. "Seeing everything from two points of view."

"I guess I never questioned it. I was always aware of my parents' differences." He gave a short, wry hoot. *"Too* aware. They were both extremely vocal people. And like a lot of children, I was called on often to referee or even to take sides."

His voice dropped a level. "It was a form of emotional blackmail, and I hated it. I think that's why going to Lake Como every year meant so much to me. *Nonno* wouldn't let either one of them within ten miles of the cabin. He said their fighting made him *pozzo,* insane."

Popping one last olive in his mouth, he considered. "It took me a long time to realize that it was the only way they knew how to communicate, and that they thrived on the turmoil. I don't think *Nonno* ever understood that."

"Yes," Lindy nodded, pushing her dish away. "Some people are like that. They need that emotional roller coaster to prove they're alive. That was the trouble with Blair."

She glanced away in distraction, irked that his name had jumped so quickly to her tongue.

"My ex-husband," she explained unnecessarily. "He wasn't happy unless he was riding faster than the speed of sound. It was exhausting. He had to stir things up just to see what would happen."

"Out of that perverse curiosity you were talking about?"

She looked at him, somehow gratified that he made the connection so readily. "Yes, but it's one thing to have it professionally and quite another with your personal relationships."

Weighing her remark, he nodded. "I agree. I guess that's why I never married. Oh, I came close once . . . or maybe twice. But at the last minute, I balked. Afraid I'd be getting a female version of your Blair."

"Well, he's not *my* Blair anymore, thank God."

"I'll drink to that," Justin smiled.

Lindy was almost embarrassed at how happy that made her. She could think of nothing to say to hide it, so she pretended to occupy herself with cleaning up the remnants of their lunch.

"What do you say?" Justin suggested when the basket was closed. "How about a swim? The sun's really hot."

"Haven't you ever heard that you'll get cramps if you don't wait an hour?"

He waved it away. "Old wives' tale. Come on." He pulled his shirt over his head. His chest was as broad and smoothly muscled as Lindy knew it would be.

"Ready?"

Taking a deep breath, she slipped off her tank top. His glance slid rapidly to her lime green maillot, and his mouth softened.

"Let's go."

They waded into the sea until the water engulfed Lindy's legs, then submerged in skimming dives. Justin was a powerful swimmer, slicing through the sea in a golden flash. Lindy watched him more than she swam.

She could barely take her eyes off him. Finally, refreshed, she paddled ashore. Squeezing water from her curls, she reclined on the towel, letting the sun blot her mind.

She felt a few tiny wet beads fall on her leg and opened her eyes a crack. Justin stood beside her, breathing a little harder from his workout. The look on his face mingled eagerness and tenderness and . . . hunger?

She swallowed tightly as he dropped down next to her. The sun in all its potency could not erase one unanswered question.

"Justin," she said, turning her head toward his.

"Yes," he murmured, slightly breathless.

"I want to ask you something. When I told you I'd been married, you seemed a little . . . surprised. I asked you about it, and you started to speak. You were wondering something. What was it?"

His face was mere inches from hers. Light smoldered in his gold-flecked eyes.

"I found it incomprehensible," he said huskily, "that any man, once he had you, would *ever* let you go."

The last traces of her resistance vanished. His arm slid around her waist, and gently, insistently, drew her close to him. His flesh, cool from the sea, inexplicably inflamed Lindy, and her hand curled around the back of his neck, pulling his lips to hers. It was a soft kiss at first, dizzying in its pliancy. But as Justin held her tighter, his mouth opened and his tongue darted electrifyingly at hers. With an internal groan, she abandoned herself to the whirl of sensation as he crushed her body against his.

She had no idea how long it lasted, ten seconds or ten minutes. There was no past hurt and no future anxiety, just the glorious, endless present. At last, reluctantly, they parted a few inches.

"*Cara mia,* you are beautiful," Justin murmured. "And I could stay here, like this, all day. But I think we should be getting back."

The sun had sneaked behind a heavy cloud, and the wind had shifted. Lindy hadn't even noticed the new chill in the air.

"Yes, I suppose we should," she said, managing no more than a hoarse whisper.

With a tug that made her muscles ache, they untangled themselves and silently set to the task of gathering their belongings and loading the raft. When they were both seated in it, their knees touched and they smiled, maintaining the contact. Within a few minutes, they were back aboard the sloop.

"Would you like to take the rudder this time?" Justin asked, deflating the raft and storing it.

At that point, Lindy trusted neither her judgment nor her strength.

"No, thanks."

"Then come sit next to me." She did, and his arm curved around her.

The sea had roughened enough to be exhilarating, and they sped on an oblique line toward the Lido. The quickened wind whipped through the halyards, and the bow spray drifted back to them in a fine mist.

"You know, I'm cured of my bad habit," he said against her ear. "I won't be asking to see you anymore at the last minute. So I want to know right now: Will you go to *Redentore* with me tomorrow evening?"

Even in her light-headed state, the name registered. *"Redentore,"* she repeated, her head leaning comfortably, fitting perfectly into the hollow between his shoulder and neck. "Isn't that a feast-day celebration of some sort?"

"Only the biggest of the season. I promise you, it'll be lots of fun."

Tilting her head back, Lindy peered at his face. His skin pulled taut over the elegant ridge of his cheekbones. His mouth was still tender from their kiss.

"As much fun as today? Do you promise that?"

Justin smiled softly, cradling her in his gaze.

"I promise."

- *9* -

THE FEAST DAY of the Redeemer dawned in a shell pink glow. Standing on her balcony, Lindy drank it in, her bare toes curling against the dewy remnants of the night. Below her, in water shaded mauve by the awakening sun, a few ambitious tradesmen ventured forth in their launches—a grocer delivering fresh produce to the hotels, an eel-fisherman bringing in his catch, a baker with large baskets of bread swaying precariously on the deck.

The last caught a glimpse of her and offered a sweeping bow and a grin. "Zuliett!" he called, then pounded his chest. "Romeo!"

Lindy knew she shouldn't encourage him, but she was in too good a mood. She waved and gave a little curtsy before slipping back inside.

Her sleep had been light, interrupted periodically by anticipation. The minute she'd noticed a softening of the shadows in her room, she'd jumped out of bed, eager to hurry the new day along. Now she glanced at the clock, slightly dismayed. It would be hours—centuries—before she would see Justin once more.

As that thought hit her, Lindy laughed ruefully at herself—what was she, sweet sixteen again? But she didn't care, didn't care one whit. Yesterday had been wonderful. And she didn't feel any burdensome chains of involvement. Quite the contrary; for the first time in years, Lindy felt free.

How to fill the day? She drew a warm, deep bubble bath and soaked in it. She rubbed a softening lotion diligently over her skin. She ordered, by Venetian standards, a huge breakfast and polished her nails while she nibbled at it. When Celine tapped tentatively on the connecting door, it was barely nine o'clock.

"You're up." She eyed the remains of sausage and eggs. "You've *been* up. Since when are you such an early bird?"

"Since they let me out of my cage." At her sister's sleepily raised eyebrow, Lindy laughed gaily. "Sunrise was beautiful. You should have seen it. I think it's going to be a glorious day."

Blinking, Celine rapidly became alert.

"Hmm. For someone who has been a confirmed night owl, you certainly are cheery. It wouldn't have anything to do with your date yesterday, would it?"

"Oh, certainly not," Lindy replied gravely, but she couldn't dull the sparkle in her blue green eyes.

Celine's mouth dropped open. "That *is* it! Pour me a cup of coffee and tell me all about it."

"What's to tell?" Lindy shrugged, knowing half her sister's fun came from dragging it out of her. "We had a good time."

"Well, what did you say? Is he married?"

"No. He came close a few times, but he's not married."

"He told you that? Without you asking? No, wait. I know you, Lindy, you wouldn't ask. Oh, that's a very good sign, if he told you of his own accord. What else?"

"Well, he told me about spending his summers with his grandfather at Lake Como, learning to sail——"

"He spoke about his childhood?" Celine's gaze widened. "That sounds serious. Men don't talk of things like that with casual dates. What else?"

"Oh, he explained why he became an architect, why Venice and restorations are so important to him."

Celine clapped a hand to her cheek. "He told you . . . ? *Melinda*. Steven and I were married almost four years before he told me *anything* like that!"

Lindy had to laugh, shaking her head fondly. "You are too much. What do you have, a little computer to figure out what that means?"

"Now don't be flip, little sister. You know darn well that a person saves certain private details and only tells them to someone who matters very much. You don't need a computer to figure out what that means."

No, she didn't. She and Justin had found it so easy to talk. It was as if each had tapped a deep, secret well within the other. The words that spilled out were pure and untainted, never having been uttered before.

"So when will you see him again?"

"Tonight. The *festa*. He asked me to go with him."

Celine jumped up.

"The *Redentore!* Of course. So what are you wearing?" Riffling through Lindy's clothes in the armoire, she clucked disapprovingly. "Why didn't you bring your good things? There's nothing here even vaguely suitable."

Lindy opened her mouth to speak, then closed it without a sound. She couldn't have explained it until now, but she no longer could wear clothes saturated with the memory of her life with Blair. And now she was too happy even to mention his name aloud.

"Oh, Lindy," Celine was moaning, "what are we going to do? There's nothing here that Tammy couldn't wear, for heaven's sake. This is a grand affair tonight; you need a real ball gown. And this being a holiday, all

the shops are closed. . . ." She shut the armoire with a
bang.

"Listen. You've got ten minutes to get dressed. Meet
me in my room. No arguments."

"But—what—"

Celine was already gone. Lindy grinned wryly in defeat and began pulling on her clothes.

For the third time that morning, Signor Adriano rolled
out another elegant brass rack. He yanked dresses off it
with ill-concealed impatience, holding each one up
briefly for the Americans' perusal.

"Perhaps the ladies see something *here* they like?" He
was thin, impeccable; his upper lip curled in perpetual
disdain.

"Oh . . ." Celine said airily, ". . . maybe that one for
my sister. And that for me."

Raising his eyebrow, he gave a slight nod and vanished with the dresses into the back of the shop.

"Celine," Lindy whispered, tugging at her sleeve.
"Let's get out of here. I don't think he'd sell the likes
of us even his dustrag."

"You think not?" Celine shook her head knowingly.
"That's just about what he's been showing us. I'll bet
my hat they're leftovers from last year's collection. Don't
you see? We're peasants, Philistines, until we prove we
have the good taste to appreciate his really scrumptious
dresses. The trick is to keep saying No until he brings
out his good stuff."

Lindy stared at her sister. "How do you know all
this?"

Celine stared back. "You used to buy designer clothes.
Don't you remember how?"

"Sure. I saw something in a magazine I liked, called
up Saks and ordered it. Lately, of course, it's been just
me and fifty other people clawing over sales in Susie's
Bargain Basement. And this is certainly no bargain basement."

She looked around at the tastefully tapestried walls,

the dark, lush carpeting. Adriano had ushered them in
with an air of reverence usually reserved for visitors to
a cathedral.

"How did we get in here, anyway?"

"Easy," Celine shrugged. "I told him we're staying
at the Danieli. So whatever we buy, he can deliver in
huge boxes with his name prominently but discreetly
displayed. You can be sure he'll pick a busy time, when
the lobby is packed—free publicity in one of the finest
hotels in Italy. Naturally he opened up for us."

Lindy glanced at her in doubt. "Come on, Celine. All
this for a few boxes?"

"Well..." Celine waved her hand. "You do have to
know the passwords. So I asked Steven who were the
three most influential men he's met here. I just happened
to drop their wives' names into the conversation with
Adriano. Simple."

"Uh-huh," Lindy grinned. "Like Machiavelli was simple."

Celine smiled and winked as the *signor* re-entered the
room.

"My mannequins," he announced, in boarding-school
English, "will show you the gowns."

Drawing back a curtain, he revealed a small stage
semicircled with mirrors. Two models appeared wearing
Celine's choices and glazed, rather bored expressions.
It took Lindy a few minutes to realize that it was part
of the job to be so bland so as to be just a fleshed-out
hanger featuring the clothes instead of the woman.

She bet that the taller one would make a good interview. This stifling of herself didn't come easily, she
could tell.

Suddenly she frowned, although on this day even her
frown had a sunny cheerfulness to it. Now where had
that thought about the model emerged from? The curiosity, the investigative spirit that had fueled her on her
radio job had resurfaced. And she'd thought it had been
sunk for good!

With a slow, secret smile, Lindy understood the

source. It was another delicious residual from yesterday. And as the models spun, as lace and satin images tripled by the mirrors swayed before her, she gave in to the flashes from yesterday, the ones that had danced around the edge of her mind all morning

In all of them, Justin: his smile — strong jaw and white teeth; his shoulders — a yard wide and molded in bronze; his eyes — gray green, spiked with gold, like different facets of the same jewel, changing, reflecting his mood, his feelings. And what had been his mood on that small island, when he switched all that intensity on her? He'd burned into her with a heat like the sun, piercing every defense she'd layered against him.

And his lips . . . so soft, yet so harshly insistent on hers. Her heart gave a thud of remembrance.

That's where the curiosity came from. All at once, she wanted to know everything about him: how he liked his eggs cooked, what he read, where he lived, what made him laugh. She felt an almost insatiable need to fill in all his blank spaces. The parts of him she did know became touchstones of her fascination: his strength, his compassion, his dedication and, yes, his vulnerability. As she mentally caressed those qualities, Lindy gradually became aware of one thing at the same time exciting and awesome.

She was very close to falling in love with him.

"Signor Adriano has spoken."

Celine's elbow nudged her none too gently, bringing her abruptly back.

"Oh . . . y—yes," she stammered, loath to leave her reverie. "What was that again?"

Nostrils pinched, Adriano smiled tightly. "I said, what do you think?"

"Oh . . . gee, I don't know. It's quite lovely. . . . Celine?"

Her sister dismissed the dress with a flick of her wrist.

"Impossible. We want something special, unique. How do you Italians say it? *Molto di moda.* Don't you have anything else to show us?"

Adriano measured them for a moment, then inclined

his sleek head, departing and returning almost immediately with yet another brass rack. This one he handled far more carefully, draping the first dress across his arm in nearly a loving way.

"This gown——"

With a sharp intake of breath, Lindy leaned forward in her seat. "That's it," she said, her eyes shining. "That's the one I want."

"I'll call Anna to model it——"

"No, no. I'll try it on. But I know it'll be just right."

It was. As Celine and Anna helped pull the yards and yards of white organza and silk over her head, Lindy began to get that special feeling that one dress in a hundred gives, that sense of perfect union between the inward person and the outward image.

She stepped onto the stage and confronted herself in the mirrors. The dress was bare shouldered, white sprigged with tiny lavender flowers. It had a small, soft ruffle at the top and bottom of the heart-shaped bodice, and a deep one at the wide hem, all lettuce-edged in orchid. Lindy twirled, and the skirt billowed gracefully.

Adriano gave his nonchalant approval, a grudging nod.

"Not bad," Celine murmured. Her voice was calm, casual, but her eyes were shouting, "Gorgeous!"

Lindy smiled.

"I'll take it."

She almost hated to change back to her street clothes, but she did, handing the gown to Adriano to press.

Celine sighed. "You'll knock Justin's eyes out of his head. Wish I could be there to see it. Oh, well. Unless . . ."

Buttoning her blouse, Lindy looked at her sister. "Unless what?"

"Listen," Celine said eagerly, "why don't you two join us? There's a big party, some of the people Steven's been working with and others. They've reserved the roof garden of our hotel. Some of them are pretty stuffy, but with you there, we'll have fun."

Lindy couldn't resist. "What? Your good friends the passwords? Stuffy?"

"Come on, now, don't tease. You can talk Justin into it."

Lindy shook her head. "Celine, he's probably made plans already. I can't ask him to change them at the last minute."

"Oh, I see. You want to be alone with him." Celine's smile was sly. "Ain't love grand?"

"It's not that," Lindy protested. "We just enjoy each other's company. And no, I don't have to be alone with him. I simply can't spring this on him at the last minute, like I told you."

She turned away, smoothing her beige linen skirt. She didn't want Celine to guess which part was truth and which was only half-truth. She really didn't need to be alone with Justin tonight. In that she was honest. She knew that wherever they went, whatever they did, all Venice would be theirs and other people no more than churches and houses and canals—a backdrop for the drama unfolding between them. But she still couldn't tell her sister that her feelings for Justin were intensifying. Whether it was because she could hardly believe it herself, or that talking about it would jinx it, or even that it was one complication she still wasn't ready to face, Lindy really didn't know. Maybe it was merely that, for now, it was a wonderful secret just for herself.

They walked out of the dressing room to the main showroom of the shop. Celine wasn't ready to concede.

"Couldn't you just ask him?" She sounded so eager, Lindy found herself wavering.

"Well . . ." Then she remembered that Ugo Gilberti was likely to be there. Instant antagonism. And if he were there, undoubtedly the vulturous Contessa D'Alente would be hovering nearby.

"I've got a great idea, Celine. You and Steven come with us. I know Justin won't mind. And we'll put a ban on business talk; nothing but fun tonight."

"I don't know what Steven——"

Lindy brushed her protests away. "It's settled. You can't waste your life on stuffy people. Now, which dress do you want?"

"Oh, I guess that mint green chiffon. I can wear my emerald earrings with it."

Lindy surveyed the gown's high neckline and conservative cut. She shook her head and flipped through the last rack.

"Aha! How about this?"

She displayed a slender, narrow-strapped tube of silk taffeta, the same brilliant green as Celine's prized earrings.

"Oh, I couldn't. Steven——"

"Steven," Lindy cut in, "will love it. It will wipe every trace of business out of his mind."

Celine bit her lip hopefully, and for a moment she seemed almost girlish.

"Do you think so?"

"I *know* so. Fun, Celine." She clasped her sister's hand and grinned in excitement. "Tonight we are going to dance and drink champagne and be the toasts of Venice, you and I."

Tossing her head, Celine agreed. "We will. For tonight, business be damned. For tonight, *l'amore!*"

While Celine's gown was being pinned for a few minor adjustments, Lindy signed her bill. The gown cost more than three weeks' salary, but she didn't care. For such a long time, her purchases had been merely utilitarian. Now...she was ready for an extravagant, exquisite costume; she was ready to start living again.

At last her sister was finished. After one more haughty nod and a brisk "Good day, ladies," from Signor Adriano, they stepped side by side into the blanketing sunshine.

"To lunch?" Lindy suggested.

"To lunch."

They set off down the *calle*. Before they had gone more than ten yards, a street urchin jumped in their path.

"Hey, lady," he said jauntily, "you want buy bang-

bang?" He pulled a string of tiny firecrackers out of the back pocket of his shorts. *"Festa* tonight. Much happy. What you say, lady?"

Lindy gave him a stern look, but he stood his ground patiently as if to say, "This is my territory, my city." She laughed at the Italian confidence already instilled in this cocky boy.

"Okay, kiddo. You made a sale."

In one motion, the boy tossed the firecrackers at her, grabbed the *lire* she offered, and dropped a *grazie* over his shoulder as he sped away.

Dubiously, Celine eyed the purchase. "You're not really going to set those off, are you?"

Lindy gave the firecrackers a saucy swing. "You never know. Tonight I might do anything."

Night came teasingly, slowly, almost reluctant to cede to Lindy's anticipation. When at last the deep wine shadows lengthened and the sun gave its last brilliant wink before dipping below the horizon, she was nearly aglow with expectation.

The festival was just beginning, and already Lindy had a lovely kaleidoscope to remember it by: Her dress arriving in a huge gray box with, sure enough, "Bottega Adriano" inscribed across the top. Inside, a surprising extra; Adriano had enclosed a handful of tiny silk violets, each surrounded by baby's-breath. She tucked them into her golden curls, wryly surmising that the designer hadn't trusted her judgment in choosing accessories for his creation.

She viewed her image in the rococo mirror, pleased with the snowy white gown flecked with lavender, her smooth bosom and arms, and a depth to her smile that had been missing too long, too long.

And at last, when the waiting was about to cause flutters, Justin appeared, so handsome in his tuxedo that her breath caught in her throat. The crisp white of his shirt emphasized the breadth of his chest, the richness of his tanned skin. Unlike many men she knew, he looked not stiff in his evening clothes, but almost regal, defined and enhanced by the smart, polished lines. His smile matched hers in liveliness, revealing a little anticipation of his own.

But best of all was the light in his eyes when he first saw her. It was bright, unfiltered by restraint, equal parts admiration and excitement, with a glint of wonder, shared by Lindy, at their good fortune in being together.

"Bel-LIS-sima!" he murmured with feeling.

Warmth flashed through her. With a giddy sense of pleasure, she let her happiness show.

He had two presents for her. The first, wrapped in layers of pink tissue was a bottle of Shalimar.

"How did you know this was my favorite?" she said, delighted. Opening it, she was unable to resist dabbing the crystal stopper behind her ears.

"My powers of deduction. I roused a perfumier friend of mine from his siesta and spent the entire afternoon sniffing at scents until I found the one that I remembered as being you."

"That's amazing. Most people can't tell the difference between scents after smelling five or six."

"I know." His smile crinkled. "After I drove my friend, his wife, and myself crazy trying to identify it, I gave up and called your sister."

So that was why Celine had been grinning all afternoon.

"Open the other."

It was a florist's box, and as she flipped back the lid, Lindy's lips parted in surprise. Inside was a small spray of miniature white roses, gathered and tied with narrow lavender ribbons.

"Oh, Justin, they're beautiful," she smiled, pinning them to her waist, knowing that was the perfect place for flowers with such old-fashioned charm. Suddenly she realized that here in Venice, on this night of a centuries-old gala, time was irrelevant. She could be surrounded by candles and lace or by arc lights and the latest designs from Milan; it didn't matter. Venice was Venice, and it had a kind of softly diffused magic about it.

She fingered lilac ribbons. "Talking to Celine again, I see."

"Yes," he admitted. "She described the color of your dress"—his voice dropped a notch—"but I never expected... You know, you could be a Venetian princess on her way to the doge's ball."

Looking at him, she gave a little laugh. "Or, to paraphrase something you said to me in the markets, I just as easily could be Lucrezia Borgia, plotting..."

Squeezing her hand, he shook his head. "No. Not tonight. Probably never, but especially not tonight."

Lindy felt the strength in his grasp. He was right. Tonight the doors were open wide, there were no shadows across her heart.

She remembered little of getting from the hotel to the site Justin had chosen for their view of the celebration. She centered on the contact between them: holding his arm as they walked to the motor launch; interlacing fingers as they sped up the wide Giudecca Canal. Clasping his hand as he ushered her from the boat to an elegant, gaily decorated barge. She was vaguely aware of Celine and Steven accompanying them, of the table for four, set with pastel yellow linen and multicolored summer bouquets, of smartly dressed people encircling them with holiday voices. But the object of Lindy's concentration was Justin's touch, his nearness. She was almost entranced by him until the first joyous pop of a champagne cork brought everything into radiant focus.

"May I have the first toast?" Justin spoke to all at their table, but he gazed only at Lindy. "To beautiful American tourists. The glories of Venice pale beside them."

His mouth twitched for Celine's and Steven's benefit, so they would take his words as gallant, continental praise; but Lindy read his deeper message. He was telling her that for once, for tonight at least, his dedication to the city, his passion for his work, was being pushed into the background—for her.

The champagne bubbles seemed to release her senses, so she was finally able to absorb her surroundings. The barge was actually a sizable open ballroom. From a central iron pole, strings of lights, unlit as yet in the last minutes of evening, formed a canopy above them.

Lindy had noted only a few of the pleasant details when a parade of waiters appeared from the dockside restaurant carrying platters aloft. They served an antipasto of baked scallops, then rice with scampi, and broiled lobster.

Lindy tasted everything, listening and joining in the breezy conversation with the others, but her attention was not on the succulent dishes before her. It kept shifting to her right, to Justin. The table was small, and casually, naturally, their knees touched underneath, a point of contact unbroken throughout the leisurely meal.

Justin, a marvelous host, had put her sister and brother-in-law at ease from the start. Celine abandoned her matchmaker role and was enjoying herself thoroughly. Steven had actually shed his serious demeanor and seemed more surprised at that than anybody, blinking, especially at his wife, in a new way. Not a word of business passed his lips.

The departing sun cast a roseate glow, tinting everything a delicate pink. With a flourish, the waiters brought the final course, the dessert, in crystal bowls.

"A sherbet of mulberries," Justin explained. "Mulberries are traditional for *La Festa del Redentore*."

It was smooth, icy, exactly the right ending for the dinner. Lindy ate between peeks at Justin, tracing his profile with her eyes. How can fingers so strong be at the same time so gentle? she wondered silently. How can eyes so deeply green have so much of the sun in them?

But aloud she said, "Tell me about *Redentore*."

"It's a thanksgiving feast," he began, again addressing them all, but looking almost constantly at Lindy. "In the late sixteenth century, a great plague gripped the city. When it finally ended, the doge ordered the building of a church and an annual commemoration of the deliverance."

Yes, oh yes, Lindy thought. How appropriate that her first true celebration in ages should be on the night remembering the rescue from a terrible plague. In that peculiar way Venice had of blending past and present, she found herself identifying totally with the joy, the relief, the unbound happiness of a four-hundred-year-old tradition.

She sipped the last of her champagne, and Justin, smiling, refilled her glass.

"So," he continued, "when night falls, the procession begins. Sometimes it seems every boat in Venice—from little *sandali* to huge *motoscafi*—join in. We will too."

"In the launch?" Celine asked.

"No." Justin smiled, savoring the surprise. "Exactly as we are; on this barge."

They all murmured in delight.

"When will the procession start?" Lindy wondered.

"Soon, *cara,* soon."

She didn't even notice Celine's eyes widening at his use of the endearment. She waited for the next magical image to appear in her kaleidoscope. As if yielding finally to her wish, the canopy of lights blinked on and the orchestra swung from dinner music to a dance tune. Right on cue, two snub-nosed workboats, freshly painted and festooned with flowers for the occasion, nudged the stern of the barge, behind the bandstand. They began moving slowly away from the pier, drifting dreamily down the canal.

"Would you like to dance?" Justin asked.

She nodded, and they moved to the center of the floor. His arm slipped around her so easily, their bodies pressed together so spontaneously, that Lindy was amazed she'd lasted so long without his touch. She closed her eyes as his cheek rested on her temple. He seemed to sigh deeply, and she smiled in contentment, smelling the faint citrus scent of his after shave.

"Know what?" he murmured against her ear.

"Mmm," she answered, too comfortable even to move her lips.

"Yesterday, sailing with you, was..." His voice trailed off, as if he were searching for elusive words. "...heavenly. I haven't been able to stop thinking about you ever since. I feel that I've known you forever, and yet you are a constant wondrous discovery to me."

Somehow his confession did not surprise her. It should, it should, she tried to convince herself. He'd practically said he...

It didn't matter. At this point, she knew his feelings as if they were her own. Their closeness had melded more than their bodies; his embrace encompassed more than her waist. It was winding around her heart.

Once the sun was gone, darkness descended quickly. The canopy of lights was lined with black velvet sky, sporting a few twinkling lights of its own making. Swaying gently in time to the music, Lindy had no idea how long they danced. She gave barely a thought to Celine and Steven, and none at all to the other passengers. Only when someone shouted, *"Chiesa del Redentore!"* did she glance around.

The Church of the Redeemer was before them, its bell tower like a minaret flooded with golden light. Laughing, singing people crowded around it, on land and water.

"Say"—Justin's interjection sounded impulsive—"we never did take that gondola ride. How about it?"

"Now?"

"Sure. Unless you'd rather stay and——"

"No, no. It sounds terrific. But how will we get off?"

"Leave it to me."

Leaning over the railing, he whistled sharply at a passing *motoscafo*. He and the pilot shouted a few words back and forth, and as soon as Lindy could gather her wrap and purse, a helpful passenger was handing her down to Justin in the smaller boat. They cuddled into the back seat as their new friends began a chorus of "Santa Lucia" in honor of a visitor from Naples.

"Happy?" Justin whispered in her ear.

If only there were words, she thought. If only she could discover the one string of letters that equaled the fullness, the totality of the happiness she felt. It was more powerful than anything she'd ever experienced. It was . . . love?

As soon as she let the word into her conscious mind, she realized it had been hovering in the background all night, like the soft music playing on the barge. And oddly, none of the panic she always associated with it was there now.

It was a matter of trust, she decided, snuggling against his shoulder. She'd put her life in his hands.

That was the difference this time, when her love was for Justin. He was worth any risk, every risk.

With the tip of his finger, he tilted her chin upward. His eyes were meltingly warm.

"I suddenly find myself," he said softly, "wanting, *needing*, to be away from everyone else. Just us in a gondola. And the gondolier had better be deaf and blind."

She could only nod. Yes, Justin, yes, yes . . .

- *10* -

IT WAS RIDICULOUSLY easy. No sooner had the launch pulled up to the steps across the canal, no sooner had Justin grasped her waist and lifted her out with a swoop that took her breath, than a gondola bobbed alongside.

"Signor?" The gondolier looked at them expectantly.

It's as if he read our minds, Lindy thought, a little giddy from the champagne. Then she realized there was no trick, no mysterious communication involved. They were open books, she and Justin. His arms still enfolded her, and she had a feeling that his look of enthrallment was mirrored on her own face. They were obviously prime candidates for a midnight boat ride.

"Si, si," Justin answered, barely taking his eyes from Lindy. Breaking reluctantly away, he stepped into the gondola and turned to help her aboard. The tenderness in his expression amazed her.

They sat on the red velvet seat, and Justin curved his arm around her. Lindy leaned lightly against him, her head resting on his shoulder. The gondolier dipped his pole into the inky canal, and they glided into the mainstream, oblivious to the celebrating crowd, the other craft plying the waters.

"Ah, yes," Justin sighed. "This is much better. I can have you all to myself. Let me look at you."

She raised her head, and his fingers gently brushed her cheek. He smiled.

"Hello, Lindy."

Her answer was little more than a whisper. "Hello, Justin."

With infinite care, he bent toward her. When his face was inches from hers, he hesitated for a second, and Lindy felt her mouth go soft in welcome. Then, with a silky touch, his lips were on hers, exploring with supple feather strokes. She relaxed, sinking into his cushioning embrace, aware of only the tingling imprint of his kisses.

Gradually, a melody filtered through to her consciousness. The orchestra barge was out of sight, but the strains of a romantic Italian tune floated toward them on the moonlit night. The gondolier hummed along, then began singing in muted tones.

Justin heard the song as well and smiled at her. "Do you know this song?" he asked, tracing the line of her jaw with his fingertips.

Her eyes locked by his, Lindy shook her head slowly.

His thumb slid in a satiny path down the side of her throat, circling the hollow at the base of her neck before sliding back up again.

"It tells of a young man, a *Veneziano,* who searches for his love. He steers his gondola through every canal, calling her name. His cry ripples through the water."

"Does he—" Lindy's voice cracked, and she swallowed to dispel the dryness. "Does he ever find her?"

"Oh, yes," Justin said softly. "When he has almost given up hope, when he most desperately needs her, like a vision, like a dream, she comes to him. Lucky man."

Listening, Lindy could understand every part of the

song, not by the words, but by the emotional flow of the music. She smiled.

"Lucky girl."

Justin nuzzled against her cheek, and Lindy closed her eyes, reveling in the rush of feeling he produced. She had been armored for so long, she'd forgotten the pure sensuous pleasure of touch. And now that she was free of her numbing protection, she was astounded by Justin's incredibly tactile manner. He was such a powerful man—both in strength and in presence. It astonished her that his kisses and caresses could be as tender as a zephyr.

Opening her eyes, Lindy gazed at the midnight sky and its lush sprinkling of stars. Part of her awakening, she knew, was due to Venice itself. It was impossible to ignore its sights and fragrances, the warm embrace of its sun and the cool kiss of its night breeze. But *Venezia*'s prodding of her senses was quickened by Justin. The stroking of his fingers, the press of his mouth sent pleasing jolts through her.

"A hundred *lire* for your thoughts," he murmured in her ear.

Her laugh was low, throaty. "I was thinking . . . how much I'm beginning to love Venetian traditions. I may never want to leave this gondola."

"Then we won't. We'll drift through the canals all night."

"Like the young man in the song?"

Cupping her chin, he lifted it as if he held the most delicate porcelain. "Not quite. I don't have to search for what I've already found."

For a moment, Lindy's heart seemed to skid and bounce in her chest. She peered at his face, etched silver by the moonlight. His tenderness had somehow intensified. His skin was stretched tight, his eyes were vehemently dark.

"*Amorosa*," he whispered hoarsely. "Sweetheart. From the first time I saw you, you've been in my mind.

'She is a diversion,' I told myself. 'Work hard, and she'll go away.' And I tried. And it didn't work."

He lowered his voice until it was barely audible. But Lindy didn't need to hear his words. Somehow, as soon as they flowed past his lips, they registered in a deeper part of her.

"You're always there. And the strangest thing is, it's like you've always been there but I just never recognized you."

His eyes smoldered. "Lindy . . ."

Justin leaned over her, wrapping his other arm around her waist and drawing her close, so close she could feel his heart thudding against her own. His lips sought hers, but this time hungrily.

And this time, he began to unleash the strength she had sensed in him from the beginning. His mouth opened, tasting her. He was pulling her closer, tighter, so that her very breathing seemed suspended. And then Lindy realized that it was not only *his* strength that held them together in a loving vise. Her own arms clasped him, and she responded to his probing kiss with a compulsion that matched his.

Justin's lips left hers and moved to her cheek, her throat, her shoulder, scalding her wherever they touched. She heard a low moan, and only when she heard it again did Lindy know it came from herself.

"Justin . . . Justin . . ." Her heartbeat throbbed in her ears, drumming his name into her soul. She felt she was whirling, intoxicated by the champagne, the gondola ride through darkened canals, and most of all, the magnificent man in her arms.

"*Mia vita,*" he whispered between kisses, "*mia amore.*" His long fingers rubbed her shoulder and as they glided down her back, Lindy found her body arching against his. Compellingly, he shifted his passionate attention to her side, stroking her down over the curve of her waist, up until his thumb nudged her breast.

Lindy breathed raggedly, as electricity seemed to arc

through her. Justin's hand was closing over her breast, and her skin was taut with desire.

"Lindy," he whispered, urgency straining his voice, "come home with me. Please...come home with me."

She nodded, a rhythmic affirmation, not trusting herself to speak. He kissed her as though he wanted to know her answer with his lips. Then he raised his head, calling directions over his shoulder to the almost-forgotten gondolier.

Her blood pounding in her ears, Lindy snuggled into Justin's arms. "Come home with me..." Unspoken, but just as clear, was the rest of his plea: "...and into my bed." It had been a long time, a very long time. She'd had no other man since Blair. She simply had squelched all her yearnings. But now...her body ached for Justin's. She could no more deny herself his touch than she could air to breathe.

The gondola veered off to a smaller canal. There was little light, with the residents of the neighborhood out enjoying the *festa*. In her dreamy state, Lindy felt as if they were wrapped in a dark, private cocoon.

As they rounded a corner, a harsh streetlight intruded. A boy standing under it flagged them with a hand-lettered sign that read, *"Fotografia."*

"Eh, signor!" he called as they approached. "I make a picture for you and pretty lady."

Raising his camera as they passed, he snapped them with a click and the pop of a flashbulb.

"What hotel you stay, lady?"

"Danieli!" Lindy answered.

"I bring soon!"

He waved jauntily and was gone. Justin looked at Lindy with a gentle smile.

"The little rogue. He knew I wouldn't let go of you long enough to chase him off." His caressing fingers brushed the length of her arm, and when he spoke, his voice held a rasp of excitement.

"We're almost there!"

She held fast to him and tried vainly to calm the flutter of her heart. They swerved into another side canal, sailing silently under a low bridge. The gondolier asked a brief question, and Justin pointed ahead to the left, to a set of steps leading out of the water.

As the gondola bumped to a stop, Justin stood up, still holding Lindy, lifting her a little as she got out. She simply could not tear her gaze from his almost incandescent profile. She barely noticed him paying the gondolier and only vaguely heard the man's *"Grazie, signor!"* Justin turned toward her and dropped a petal-like kiss on her lips.

"Here we are, *cara*."

His key scratched in the lock, and in a moment they were in a dim hallway. Clutching Lindy's hand, he started up the narrow staircase, drawing her along, seemingly as much with his anticipation as with his strong fingers. After a few steps, she gathered her skirt over her arm, her feet flying to keep up with him.

"Wait!" she gasped, laughing, as they reached the first landing. "No fair. Your legs are longer than mine."

"Ah, so they are. Well, we'll even things up."

Before she could reply, he had scooped her into his arms and began climbing, with Lindy nuzzling his shoulder.

"This is where I live in Venice," he said at last, letting go of her legs and easing her down his body. He paused a moment, and Lindy detected a trace of nervousness in him, ardor that was surprisingly—touchingly—restrained. He unlocked the door and switched on a lamp. With slightly tremorous steps, Lindy entered his apartment.

It was a beamed attic room, papered in a blue-and-cream print, not nearly as formal as hers at the Danieli. It was charmingly comfortable, inviting. Justin removed his jacket and loosened his tie. Suddenly a little shaky herself, Lindy put her wrap and purse on a carved chair.

"Come," he beckoned, smiling, leading her to the lace-curtained French doors. "I want you to see this."

He flung the doors open, and they stepped out onto a small balcony, railed in wrought-iron, hung with fragrant oleander. The rooftop view of Venice glowed here and there with the night's festivities. Far below, a ribbon of moonlight shimmered on the canal.

"Oh, Justin! Oh, it's the most beautiful sight."

"Yes, and—look there!"

The opaque sky flickered. Starbursts of red and gold and blue spread over each other, followed by a muffled "Boom!" Standing behind her, Justin encircled her waist with his arms. Lindy rested against him, reveling, if faintly shivering, in his embrace, only half watching the fireworks.

"That signals the official end of *la festa*. But people will go on celebrating, in their own ways, all night." He leaned closer, his words whisper-soft in her ear. "For some, *amorosa*, the night has just begun."

Slowly, Lindy turned to face him. Even in the shadowy darkness, his eyes radiated a warmth that stole her breath. Without a sound, moving as one, they went back inside.

He stopped in the middle of the dimly lit room, cupping her chin, searching her uptilted face, smiling as he read her answer. With careful patience, his fingers trailed down her back, unfastening her dress. He took a step away from her, and it dropped around her feet. For heart-stopping seconds she stood, immobile, in her silk and lace underclothes. Then with trembling arms, he picked her up, carrying her to a deep alcove, to his bed.

The sheets beneath the coverlet were cool and smooth. Lindy reclined against thick pillows, and Justin sat on the edge of the bed beside her. He bent to kiss her, a deep, soothing avowal that gradually caught fire and finally blazed as they clutched hungrily at each other.

Her pulse racing, Lindy felt his hand slide down over her hip and back up again, circling her stomach, reaching sensuously under the silk and lace. A liquid heat melted through her.

"Ah, Lindy..." Justin groaned. Standing up, breathing hard, he roughly began to unbutton his shirt.

"Here..." Lindy whispered hoarsely, getting to her knees, "let me..."

Her fingers hurried over his buttons, and as he shrugged quickly out of the shirt, she spread her hands over his chest, exploring, massaging. He edged toward her, but with light pressure, she held him off.

"Wait..."

The staccato beat of her heart vibrated down to her fingertips. Gazing at Justin, watching his chest rise and fall unevenly, Lindy reached around to unhook her bra. It fell away, and she heard the sharp intake of his breath.

"My God, Lindy," he whispered shakily. "You are so beautiful..."

He stood up. Moonlight streaming through the open doors surrounded him with a luminous aura. His eyes never leaving her, he kicked off his shoes and peeled off the rest of his clothes, finally kneeling with her, naked.

With a shuddering sigh, Justin clasped her to him. The shock of his flesh against hers sent sparks through Lindy. His hands swirled over her, and his lips followed the same trail. Twining her fingers through his dark hair, she directed his kisses, until she thought she would go ecstatically mad.

"Justin... Justin—I want you."

Lindy felt his blood surge wildly and heard his stifled moan. Pulling her down on the bed, he rolled over her, holding himself off with muscle-corded arms, his face inches from hers. His eyes flared with intensity.

"Do you mean it, *cara?* Because Lindy... my darling ...I want you like I've never wanted any other woman. But I want *all* of you. Lindy, every part of you. Do you understand?" His concentration was almost fierce. "All! Not just your body—your mind... your heart... your soul."

She could think of no answer as profound as her feelings for him. Her mouth formed a silent, reverberating Yes.

With a sure motion, she tugged off the last silken

barrier against him. His cherishing hands skimmed her every taut curve and swell. Lindy crushed her mouth to his, fervently trying to slake their mutual thirst.

Still, he withheld a measure of his desire—instinctively, Lindy knew—from a need to protect her. She would have none of it. She'd had glimpses of his passionate power too often. If he was to be hers, she wanted every bit of him too.

And magically, the quest of her kiss, the persuasion of her flesh, seemed to draw it from him, until he could resist no more. Their feverish bodies joined in a pulsating rhythm.

"Oh, Justin . . ."

"Lindy, my love . . ."

A torrent of sensations swept through her, gathering, mounting, cresting . . . finally washing in shock waves over her. Lindy closed her eyes and floated with them, hugging Justin tightly until she slowly drifted back into her limp body.

She breathed deeply, inhaling a sultry scent of oleander and moonlight and spent passion. A languid smile crossed her deliciously bruised lips. This, she decided, was where she wanted to stay forever. . . .

Lindy's eyes fluttered open, and she blinked, disoriented. But only for a moment. Then she stretched voluptuously, remembering where she was.

"Hey," an affectionate voice murmured in her ear, "you're awake."

Justin was propped up on one elbow, watching her with incredible tenderness. Laughing, she rolled into his arms, and they lay with their heads side by side on the pillow.

"I must have fallen asleep. What time is it?"

Justin glanced at the night table behind him.

"Almost three. Will your sister be worried about you?"

"I don't think so." Lindy suppressed a giggle. "From the way Steven was staring at her all evening, I'd say she hasn't had time to give me a second thought."

"Aha!" Stroking her cheek, Justin grinned. "You mean because her mind was occupied with something like this?"

Closing her fingers around his, she brought them to her lips. "Something like this," she agreed in a whisper, knowing her eyes were still soft from the rapture of it. Then his loving expression drove away all thoughts of Celine, and Lindy kissed his forehead, his cheeks, his chin.

"*Ah, cara,* you look like an angel," he murmured, when she leaned back on the pillow. "Spun gold and white marble. And with a look in your eyes that could turn a man to jelly."

"That doesn't sound very angelic to me," she said dryly, poking him.

"You're right. You're much too bewitching." His long fingers framed her face. "Have you cast a spell on me, Lindy Thorne?"

In answer, she pressed her open lips to his. There was a dreamy intimacy to their kiss now, she realized, more sweetness than spice, born from what they had shared.

"If any spells were cast," she said, her eyes moist with feeling, "it was you who did it. I don't know how. I fought like hell not to let you get to me, but it didn't do a bit of good. I have never, *ever* felt like I did tonight. I've been only existing, Justin; you brought me *alive.*"

Gathering her into his arms, Justin held her snugly. "Lindy, *amorosa mia.* I was wrong; you cannot be marble and gold. You are much too soft, too warm. And you may have tried to deny it, but there is one thing I have never doubted: Life burns more brightly in you than in anyone I've ever known."

He tilted her head gently back, and his voice was a velvet murmur. "I meant it when I told you I wanted all of you. You see, my darling, I can't divide my affection. I give it all or I give none. The problem is, I have always been afraid to ask for the same total commitment . . . and afraid to settle for anything less."

His hands caressed the plane of her back. "I can hardly

believe it," he whispered, with something close to awe in his tone. "But I have found someone capable of returning my total, unbounded . . . infinite . . . love."

His stroking hands pressed harder, and his body signalled new desire for her. As they began the ritual, this time slowly, with a sense of wondrous discovery. Lindy was surprised to find a hot, exultant tear trickling down her cheek.

- *11* -

SHE CLOSED THE door quietly behind her and leaned against it. Was this the same hotel room she'd left only—what?—twelve hours ago? It looked oddly different until she realized that it was she who had changed, dramatically.

Smiling, Lindy moved to the tall windows and cast aside the heavy draperies. Stepping back in a pool of morning sun, humming snatches she remembered from the gondolier's song, she reached around to undo her dress. Laughter bubbled up inside her as she thought of the last hands that helped her out of it. She knew it was crazy, but she could still feel the imprint of his special touch on her body.

Even now she couldn't believe how wonderful everything had been. There was more, much more to Justin than she had ever dreamed. True, she had sensed the complexities in him almost from the first, his Old-World manners and New-World energy, his incredibly magnetic power and awesome tenderness. But she had been bowled over by the depth of his feeling, his capacity for giving, his limitless pleasure in her happiness. This was a man, Lindy knew, to whom halfway was no way at all.

In the early moments of dawn, after their second, exquisite lovemaking, they'd begun to talk about all sorts of things—what they liked and hated; what made them laugh; and what moved them to tears. And when the dawn ripened, when the first rays of sun crept through the open French doors, they had dressed in their superfluous finery and gone to find breakfast. The *trattoria* they chose faced a fountained *piazza*. Lindy smiled now, remembering how the apricot sunlight sparkled on the dancing water, reflecting her happiness, and how, gazing at the fountain, she suddenly had been filled with an amazing sense of completeness—physically, mentally, and emotionally. The discovery had almost caused her to weep with joy. She hadn't understood until then how fragmented she had become . . . and was no longer.

"That's right," she said softly to the awakening city outside her window. "You'd hardly recognize me. I'm a whole person now."

All over Venice, Sunday morning church bells pealed their delight. It occurred to Lindy that one day had faded into the next and she'd had slept only a few minutes, cradled in Justin's arms.

She might never be able to sleep any other way, she thought, smiling to herself. But even as she did, she felt a drowsiness overtaking her. She slipped into her ivory silk nightgown and crept into bed. Her head sank into the soft pillow, and she closed her eyes.

A persistent knocking broke through her dreams.

"Y—yes?" she called, half groggy.

"Lindy?" Celine poked her head through the connecting door. "Listen, I wouldn't disturb you . . . but the hall porter has been trying to get you and was too polite to beat on your door."

"Mmmm," Lindy protested. "Let me sleep s'more."

"Normally, I would," Celine replied cheerfully, stepping into the room, "but not today. *Wait* until you see what's come for you!"

Sighing, Lindy raised up, slumber still heavy on her eyelids.

"What?"

Waving her arm dramatically, Celine drew the porter and an assistant inside. Lindy's mouth dropped open, and she blinked, suddenly alert.

"Whaaaaat?"

Each man carried two huge baskets, filled to overflowing with flowers—roses of every hue, carnations, daisies, and some that Lindy didn't even recognize. Four explosions of color, as joyful as the fireworks last night.

"Oh, my—Is there a card?"

The porter handed it to her with a flourish and, motioning for his assistant, left. With fingers that trembled slightly, Lindy opened the tiny envelope.

A few of Mother Nature's better creations—for the best one of all.

Love,
J.

She stared at the words written in Justin's bold, sweeping hand. Happiness welled up inside her and spilled out in a smile.

"Hmm!" Crossing her arms, Celine gave a victorious smirk. "I can just guess who bought out an entire florist's shop today. That must have been *some* gondola ride."

Breathing deeply, Lindy lay back on the pillows.

"It was."

Celine clapped her hands together, a punctuation of her glee. "Oh, I just knew it! The first time I saw that man, I said to myself, 'He is *perfect* for Lindy.'" She buried her face in one bouquet after another. "And such a sense of style! All these beautiful flowers—Of course, I wouldn't ask what he wrote on that card. I'm sure it's much too personal. . . ."

She looked up hopefully, but Lindy simply gave her an enigmatic wink, and Celine shrugged in resignation. "Well, whatever he wrote, I'm sure it's romantic and lovely.... Listen, just tell me one thing: Is he as terrific as he is gorgeous?"

Lindy rested on her elbow, considering for Celine's benefit.

"You know, he really is. Even more than I imagined. We talked for hours, about everything under the sun. And the more we talked, the more I knew I l—liked him."

She glanced up swiftly to see if Celine had caught her stammer. Every passing moment reinforced her certainty that she was in love with Justin, yet Lindy wasn't ready to tell her sister. She had to get used to the feeling before she could frame it with words.

"We had a wonderful time," she finished lamely, thankful that Celine was too engrossed in the flowers to have noticed her slip.

"I'm so glad, hon. Wasn't the feast day celebration spectacular? I think Steven and I were the only people in Venice who didn't stay up all night. Although believe me, two A.M. *is* practically all night for Steven. I'll bet Justin took you somewhere fabulous. One of those great restaurants—or no, an elegant party at a *palazzo* on the Grand Canal, right?" She raised a quizzical and undevious eyebrow for confirmation.

As Lindy dropped her gaze to the florist's card still in her hand, it occurred to her that she was ludicrously close to a blush.

"Uh, well... actually, we went... to his apartment."

There was no point in lying. And besides, she realized with a wry smile, her cheeks were not flushing because of her disclosure to Celine. It had more to do with remembering that that deliciously wanton creature in Justin's apartment had been her. More composed, she looked up at her sister, who stared at her with rounded eyes.

"You mean you were—all night you——"

"Celine," Lindy said gently, leaning forward. "It was beautiful. Really."

"Well." Celine smiled briefly, regaining her poise. "You're an adult. You know what you're doing, I guess." She was picking at a yellow carnation, and Lindy could see she was grappling with her mother-hen instincts. "It just—just seems so sudden for you to be *that* involved. I mean—good grief, Lindy—only a few days ago you could hardly make up your mind to go on one date with him."

"Celine . . ."

"I know what it was," she blurted. "It was that champagne, wasn't it!"

Celine was so earnest, so sure. In spite of herself, Lindy felt a ripple of mirth, and she couldn't contain it.

"I'm serious, Melinda."

Still laughing, but shaking her dark blonde curls contritely, Lindy got up and went to give her sister a little squeeze of affection.

"I know you are. It just struck me funny to think of myself as a Victorian maiden, led astray by demon spirits." She patted Celine's cheek playfully. "This is the modern age, sister dear. Nobody has to get us drunk anymore."

"I guess you're right," Celine admitted, somewhat mollified. "It's just—well, frankly, I thought that you'd be safe, that your Signor DiPalma was—oh, I don't know—more traditional, I suppose."

Stepping back, Lindy faced her squarely. "Celine. Don't confuse the man with the architect. He's interested in preserving old buildings, not outdated ideas of seduction." She grinned to dull the sharpness in her tone. "It was mutual consent. No handcuffs, honest."

Gradually, Celine's worried frown receded. She sighed, managing a weak smile. "I'm sorry; I'm really not as scandalized as I sounded."

"Oh, thank God!"

"Don't be flip, Lindy. Look, I know you don't like me to refer to the past, but the truth of the matter is I think you of all people should be very careful of a summer romance. You may wake up four years later and find out that you've got something very much unlike what you bargained for."

For the first time, Lindy regretted the dolorous pride that had kept her from revealing the true cause of her broken marriage—Blair's infidelities and lack of love. She'd told the few who deserved an explanation that she could no longer stand the shallowness of their lives. Celine had stifled her skeptical surprise and loyally said nothing. And now she was making unfounded comparisons.

"Justin's different," Lindy insisted.

"I hope so," Celine answered sincerely. "And I hope you understand that I'm not questioning what you do with your personal life. . . . Lindy, don't you see? I feel sort of . . . guilty for pushing Justin at you. All I wanted was for you to have a little harmless vacation fun. So much bad has happened to you in the last few years, and I just wanted you to enjoy yourself. But I never *dreamed* you'd get so . . . involved so fast. The very *last* thing I want is to see you hurt again."

Touched by her concern, Lindy hugged her sister.

"Celine . . . thank you. But don't worry about me; I really do know what I'm doing."

"Okay. I hope so. . . . Listen, I have to get back and see what Tammy and Todd are up to. They're probably hungry, as usual. And *you* must be starved. You missed lunch."

Glancing at the clock, Lindy was amazed to see the hands at three thirty. "My gosh! I had no idea it was so late. I've got to hop in the tub."

"Should I order from room service for you? Or do you want to eat with us later?"

Halfway to the bathroom, Lindy turned to watch her sister's reaction as she told her, "Justin said he'd call. We're going out for dinner."

Pausing a moment, Celine seemed to study Lindy's face. Finally she sighed in good-humored defeat.

"Have a nice time."

"I will," Lindy called over her shoulder, waving as Celine went gratefully back to her less troublesome family.

She really should tell Celine everything, Lindy mused as she sprinkled a liberal dose of bath salts in the water. After all, her sister *did* worry about her.

She replaced the cap thoughtfully. Celine assumed her relationship with Justin was a summer fling. Could she be right? Lindy shook her head vehemently. No. Not possible.

For the first time it dawned on her that only a few days remained on their scheduled stay, and she caught her breath sharply. Leave Venice and Justin? Leave the man who had unlocked her heart and soul? Never!

Shaken, she sat on the edge of the tub. For all her apprehensions, for all her fears of complicating her life again, she knew, with clarity so precise it astounded her, that she had to stay with him, follow him wherever he went. Nothing less would even come close to satisfying her.

But how would *he* feel about that?

The jangling telephone roused her just in time to prevent the tub from overflowing. She quickly shut off the water and rushed to pick up the receiver.

"Hello?"

"Signorina Thorne? One moment for Signor Di Palma." Her grip on the telephone tightened until she heard the gratifying sound of his voice.

"Lindy?"

"Yes! Hi."

"Sorry . . . have another bad connection. . . . Just heard . . . radio . . . telephone workers might strike in Venice too."

There was a fearsome crackle and then silence.

"Justin?"

"Yes. I can hear you fine now."

"Me too. I mean, I can hear you fine too."

They both paused, and Lindy felt her pulse beat in her throat.

"How are you today, *cara?*" Justin asked softly at last.

"Oh, just great! Wonderful, fantastic, terrific . . . Take your pick." Her words came in a rush, and Lindy realized she'd been holding her breath.

"I'm so glad. Did you get some sleep?"

"Uh-huh. And guess what I woke up to? Half the flowers in Venice crammed into my room. They're absolutely glorious, and I can't tell you how special they made me feel."

"I would have sent five times that many, but it is a Sunday, you know. And in my happy state of mind, I could only stand to fight with one florist to open up. But, Lindy"—his mellow voice tingled in her ear— "there aren't enough flowers in all Italy to let you know how special I really think you are."

She closed her eyes, letting his tenderness sink in.

"Oh, Justin . . . I'll never be able to tell you what last night meant to me."

"Well, I'll give you a chance to try." There was a hint of a grin in his tone. "Have you eaten anything since breakfast?"

"No." She closed her eyes, remembering the steaming cups of *caffelatte,* thick sweet rolls, and intimate smiles they had shared.

"How about a drink and an early dinner? Afterwards we can walk along the Zattere. It's beautiful at sunset. Besides, I want you to see my latest project. We're restoring a big, old, dark yellow warehouse, converting it into apartments and small shops. I want you to know all about my work, to share in it."

"Sounds exciting! When will you be here?"

"Fifteen minutes."

"Wait," she laughed in protest. "I need at least thirty. I was just about to get in the tub."

"In that case, I'll be there in five."

Their laughter mingled over the wire. When Justin spoke again, she almost had to stop breathing to hear.

"Lindy?"

"Yes..."

"I—There's so much we have to talk about, *amorosa mia.*"

"Yes, I know."

"I'll see you in half an hour."

"Yes... *ciao.*"

Lindy hurried, singing, through her bath. After a moment of thought, she decided to wear the white eyelet sundress she'd had on that first night in St. Mark's Square. It seemed somehow symbolic.

She didn't bother to sit at the dressing table while she dabbed on a bit of lip gloss, but merely leaned toward the mirror. As she straightened up, she noticed that her eyes held a gleam that no makeup could improve upon, and her skin looked buffed to a glow. She winked at her reflection just as the phone rang.

"Hello?"

"Signorina Thorne? There is a gentleman——"

"I'll be right down."

She raced around to find her purse, hopping from one foot to the other putting her shoes on. The rascal, she thought, grinning, he's early. He must have decided he couldn't wait after all. The idea of his eagerness delighted her.

The elevator seemed interminably slow. Lindy shifted her weight and smoothed nonexistent wrinkles from her skirt. At last the door opened onto the lobby. Barely able to resist running, she rushed out to meet her love.

"Hello, darling."

The voice behind her was a low, familiar purr. Even as she spun around, yearning for Justin's welcoming arms, some unidentifiable, jarring note nagged at her. As she completed her turn, she knew what it was.

The voice belonged to Blair.

Lindy was cemented to the spot where she stood, nearly numb with shock. It had been almost two years since she'd seen him, but he looked completely unchanged. His perpetually sun-bleached hair fell in the same casual, expensively cut angles. He wore his trade-

mark, an unlined cream linen jacket, sleeves pushed up
on tennis-tanned forearms. An open-necked shirt, tailored jeans, designer sunglasses completed his traveling
clothes.

He shrugged at the bags at his feet. "I just got in."

Lindy felt a clammy hand at her throat and realized
that it was hers. Overshadowing all her stupefaction was
a bristling annoyance that, after two years, he had been
able to read her mind. It was an invasion of her privacy.
She had an irrational urge to laugh and flee, but nothing
seemed to work—not her mouth, not her legs. She
wasn't even sure her heart was beating.

As Blair watched her, a sardonic smile curved across
his face.

"Melinda, darling, I expected you to be surprised, but
don't you think this pillar-of-salt routine is a bit much?
I thought we parted as friends, *très civilisé* and all that."

Lindy tried to respond. Her mind was shrieking "Go
away!" but nothing escaped the stricture of her throat.

"Well," Blair sighed. "I realize this prescription is
more suited to Sleeping Beauty than Lot's wife . . . but
what the hell."

Theatrically, he swept his arms around her and bent
her back in a swashbuckling kiss. To Lindy, his lips felt
like lead. But he caught her off-balance, and she clung
to his neck to break her fall, finally twisting her mouth
away.

"Blair!" she managed to gasp. Suddenly she froze
while still in his viselike clutch, as an icy foreboding
crawled along her back. Her head snapped around in
time to see the shattered glare that confirmed it.

Justin stood immobile, only ten feet away, his fists
in white-knuckled balls at his side. Gradually, his face
chilled into a mask. He spun and stormed out.

Lindy struggled against the lock of Blair's arms and
finally recovered her voice.

"Justin—Wait!"

The sound seemed faraway, weak and foreign to her
ears. She broke from Blair and went flying across the

lobby, mindless of the appalled gawking that followed her.

"Wait, wait," she called over and over as she ran outside, but Justin's loping stride and his fury had already carried him out of sight. She turned left and right, frantically searching for him.

A hand touched her elbow.

"My God, Melinda," Blair murmured, glancing around in mild annoyance. "You're making an absolute spectacle of yourself."

"Leave me alone!" she cried, recoiling. "I've got to find Justin!"

"I *know*, and so does the entire *piazza* by now."

They were at the edge of St. Mark's Square. She hadn't been aware of coming that far, and she probably *was* creating a scene. More than a few people were giving her quizzical stares.

"Go away," she muttered distinctly. "I've got to find someone and explain."

"Ah . . . the fellow you were bellowing after. Who was it? Johnson?"

Lindy gave him an abrupt, withering look. "Justin."

Even as she spoke his name, she pictured his devastated expression, his tempestuous glower. Her heart wrenched. Why, oh why had Blair picked the moment Justin had walked into the hotel to begin his antics? She knew what it must have looked like—the emotional reunion of two former lovers.

Betrayal.

Stifling a groan, she pressed her hand to her temple. "Blair, you have the most rotten sense of timing."

"Oh? . . . Ohhhhh, now I see. A new beau. And he stalked off in . . . jealousy? Why, Melinda, how quaint!"

"You make everything sound so vile," she snapped.

"I'm wounded to the quick. And after I came all this way to see you!"

"Why *did* you come here? What do you want from me?"

He gripped her elbow. Lindy again tried to shake him off, but his hold was more forceful now.

"I'd be delighted to tell you all about it, my dear, but not standing here like some bizarre tourist attraction. Let's go to Harry's and have a drink."

"No. I'm not having any drink with you."

"All right, all right. But at least let's get out of this Godawful heat."

"No. I'm going back to my room, and I don't ever——"

"Look"—Blair's lip curled in a way that Lindy recognized only too well—"why don't you sit down for five minutes? Who knows?—maybe your Mr Huff'n Puff will steam by and you can do your explaining. And meanwhile, I will gladly oblige you by doing some of my own."

Biting her lip, Lindy glanced morosely around the square. Would Justin have gone home to his apartment? Somehow she didn't think so, with the sheets probably still scented by her perfume and him thinking that she and Blair...Maybe he *was* walking off his anger and hurt.

"Okay, I'll stay. But only five minutes."

They found a bench in the shaded colonnade of the Doges' Palace. Lindy placed herself a careful six inches away from Blair and folded her arms, constantly scanning the crowded *piazzetta*.

"Well, I was in Monte Carlo," Blair began, friendly and nonchalant. As always, he was denying her feelings when they didn't match his own. Same old Blair.

"...if you must know," he was saying, "having a horrendous fight with a Brazilian actress, when who should saunter into Jimmy's but Bibi Rasmussen. You remember her...blonde, Nordic type, her old man's an exporter—salted cod, I think."

The woman at the *Patria Grande* reception—of course. Grimly, Lindy recalled her relief at not being recognized by good old Bibi, who clearly excelled at these cunning games.

"Anyway, she tells me that she was at some sort of

boring cocktail party in Venice when she happened to see none other than my ex-wife. I said to myself, 'Melinda? At a *cocktail party?* This is a marvel I can't afford to miss.' So I hopped the next flight, and here I am."

She glared at him. "That's what you wanted to tell me? That's why you came?"

"My dear. The idea of you with the dreaded martini in your hand was simply irresistible. Why, that gin-soaked olive was what broke up our marriage, or so Bibi said she'd heard."

Lindy jumped to her feet.

"How dare you," she said coldly. "How dare you say that! You know very well what broke up our so-called marriage. And it wasn't any damned olive!"

Wheeling, she stalked down the Riva degli Schiavoni. Same old Blair, all right. Same old unconcerned, acid-tongued——

"Wait."

He grabbed her arm and spun her around to face him. "Just wait, will you?"

"No! Take your hands off me!"

"Melinda . . ."

"I said No!"

". . . I'm sorry."

The words caught her completely off guard. She stared at him open-mouthed, as stunned as if the words had popped out of the gilded angel on top of the campanile. Blair *never* apologized, not even sarcastically. But now . . . there was actually a vague note of contrition in his tone.

"I didn't mean to screw things up for you . . . although that does seem to be one of my specialties. . . ."

Yes . . . yes, it did seem that way. Achingly, she remembered the look in Justin's eyes when he saw Blair's arms around her—startled hurt turning into white-hot anger. His words of the night before tumbled through her mind: ". . . can't divide my affection . . . give it all or give none . . . *Amorosa mia* . . . want *all* of you . . . all or none . . ."

His litany of love. Transformed by Blair's callous insensitivity into a mocking reminder that Justin needed—demanded—total commitment. He had opened his innermost self to her, the private sanctuary of his soul that he had allowed no one else to see. And now he thought she had desecrated his trust. She had to find him.

Blair's hand still clutched her arm. She pried his fingers away.

"Let go of me. I'm leaving."

He raised an amused eyebrow. "To throw yourself into the canal?"

Once Lindy would have shrunk from his sarcasm; now she merely shook her head in disgust. "It's all a grotesque joke to you, isn't it? You don't care that you may have ruined a good thing for me as long as you can cut it to pieces with your famous rapier wit. Now someone I...care about deeply is gone, and it's all your fault."

"Please, Melinda. No melodramatics. Who was he anyway?"

Who was he? Someone her ex-husband would consider an alien creature: an unselfish, cherishing man; one who aroused her dormant senses, who freed her from the prison of fear that Blair had helped build.

Anger twisted Lindy's mouth and spilled out in a bitter stream. "It's your fault! You're not happy unless you're making me miserable. You have to ruin everything for me, everything! Why did you have to come here? Why can't you once and for all leave me alone!"

"Melinda..."

Slapping away the hand he offered, she turned and began to stumble back up the quay, as acrid tears stung her eyes. She caromed off gaping tourists, blindly seeking some haven from the terrible bleakness she felt. When at last she stopped, her head spinning, her breath coming in a ragged pant, Lindy found herself at the Danieli, in the lobby...the very place where...

Smothering a sob, she fled to the solitude of her room, to collapse into her pain.

- *12* -

"I AM SORRY, *signorina*. There is no answer."

"Oh . . . would you please let it ring a little longer?"

But there was still no reply, only a taunting double buzz.

"Sorry."

Lindy blew out an exasperated breath. "Well, have you found out if there's something wrong with the line?"

"Not yet, *signorina*. It is being checked."

"They've been checking it since yesterday evening." She compressed her lips, trying not to snap at the hotel operator. "What about the telephone workers' strike? Has it hit Venice yet? Is that the problem?"

"We have not heard. Sorry, *signorina*."

Sorry. It seemed everyone was apologizing these days.

"All right. I'll try again later."

Lindy hung up the telephone, rubbing at the lines that furrowed her forehead. Where could Justin be? She had

been calling him regularly since the night before, re-
peating again and again the number that was by now
carved as deeply in her as the marks of worry etched in
her face. There had been no answer.

Where could he be? Almost twenty-four hours had
passed since the horrid scene with Blair. Lindy clenched
her fists. Never in her life had she felt more like hitting
someone. Because of Blair she was pacing in her room,
her stomach churning with anxiety and frustration. And
Justin was out there somewhere in the city, convinced
that Lindy had lied to him.

But where? With a friend, maybe...someone he'd
done a restoration for. What was the name of the man
at the party? Signor...? On the Calle...? Her mind
was a maddening blank. The only other people she'd met
who were friends of his were the American heiress Mrs.
Renniger and Madame Delphine. She wasn't yet des-
perate enough to go flying off in search of Justin like
some lovesick teen-ager, especially to such worldly,
poised women as those two.

Besides, a nasty thought nagged at her, what if she
found him with one of them? Immediately she caught
herself up. After all, she had chided Celine for antiquated
sexual assumptions. Men could have beautiful female
friends who were not necessarily also lovers. She could
accept that. Then she realized that it didn't help. Lindy
wanted to be the one to whom he fled for solace in bad
times. Her spirits sank even lower.

And since she was now discouraged enough, another
grim possibility was born: Perhaps he had been home all
this while and was simply refusing to pick up the receiver,
knowing she was at the other end. Perhaps he wouldn't
ever want to speak to her. Tears formed as she imagined
him in his sweet-smelling attic room. Their love had
filled it with whispered promises and gentle cries. What
was the silence saying to Justin now?

Her head beginning to pound, Lindy sank onto the
chaise longue and stared listlessly out the window. For
once, the sun was hidden, shrouded by dirty white

clouds. It was one minor thing to be thankful for. She wouldn't have been able to stand the cheery sunshine. Not today; not with the memories of their night together, of Justin's laughter and his touch, of the thrill of her response to him, still vibrant in her mind.

"It's not fair," she whispered. "It can't end so quickly, so stupidly... when it's only started."

And the most chilling thought of all: Maybe he had left Venice, driven away by what he assumed was her emotional dishonesty. Groaning, she slumped against the cushions. She'd *never* find him, she'd——

The telephone bell startled her and Lindy bolted upright, grabbing the receiver. "H—Hello?"

"Signorina Thorne? One moment please."

Lindy's pulse was pounding so hard she was afraid she wouldn't hear the voice on the line. "Hello?" she repeated expectantly.

"One is supposed to say *Pronto,* Melinda. When in Venice, and all that..."

Her hopes thudded in two words, "Oh. Blair."

"Well, I didn't think you'd turn cartwheels, but you might show a little civility."

"Listen, I don't want to talk to you, and I don't want to tie up the line. Good-b——"

"Wait. I'm not calling to be ugly. I just wanted to know if you found your temperamental Italian."

"No, I haven't, thanks to you."

"Melinda, I said I was sorry. Remember? I know you heard me because you almost fell over from the shock of it."

"Yes, well, it was a facet of you I'd never had the honor of seeing before." When she realized what she'd done, Lindy wanted to bite her tongue. She'd let him draw her into their old pattern of trading barbs, a game in which he was the undefeated champion, secure in the knowledge that she was no match for him. She wasn't going to let him get away with it.

"Actually, Blair, your glib apologies don't interest me one bit."

"How mortifying. I'm beginning to learn what rejection is. And just when I'm trying so gallantly to make things up to you."

"Oh, really? Well, try erasing yesterday. That's the only way you could possibly make things up to *me.*"

"Anything to ease this burden of guilt. Just tell me how, for God's sake, how?"

Ignoring the heavy coating of irony, she considered Blair's question. It dawned on her that the most convincing way to explain everything to Justin might be to have Blair do it—if she could trust him not to create more havoc.

"Blair," she said suspiciously, "are you serious? Do you really want to help me?"

"Oh God, yes. Anything, my dove, anything short of voluntary castration."

"Cut the sick jokes. Will you help me or won't you? A simple Yes or No."

"Okay. Yes."

"All right. Now listen." Briefly, she related her idea. "What do you say?"

"A mere *bagatelle* . . . with a string attached."

"I knew it."

"Now, now . . . a painless one, I assure you. Your sister and brother-in-law have graciously accepted my invitation to dinner"—Lindy grimaced. The traitors— "and I'd love for you to come too. It'll be perfectly safe, Melinda, with two chaperones in a very public restaurant. Not even your volatile Italian could misunderstand."

"Damn it, Blair——"

"I know, I know. I'm sorry. See how easily that's coming to me? Soon it'll be tripping off my tongue every other sentence."

"Oh, Lord."

"All right, you want serious? Here's serious: Come to dinner. Fill me in on all the details. I'll be glad to do my part to soothe Italian-American relations."

As irritated as she was by his maneuvering, Lindy was more anxious to clear up the misunderstanding. She still had reservations about Blair's sincerity, but at this point . . . She shrugged fatalistically. She hadn't done any good on her own, and her choices were alarmingly limited. If only she could reach Justin!

"It's against my better judgment . . . but all right, I'll go. On the condition that you tell me now where we're eating so I can leave a number in case . . . anyone . . . tries to call me."

"Of course. We'll be at Quadri's in Piazza San Marco. The regular chef is on vacation and guess who's replacing him? Paolo, from Cesare's in Rome. Remember him?"

She deeply resented his reference to another time, another Lindy. At this moment she wished she had no memories in common with Blair Talbot.

"Yes, yes, I remember," she said quickly to keep him quiet. "What time?"

"Nine."

"All right. Good-bye."

"It's *ciao*, darling. *Ciao*."

That night, before they joined Steven and Blair in the lobby of the hotel, Lindy filled Celine in on exactly what had happened the day before and her reason for agreeing to dine with Blair, though she left out the miserable fear she'd felt, as well as the innumerable and fruitless phone calls she'd made.

" . . . so he promised to try to explain to Justin. But as usual, he had to extract his pound of flesh first. I want to be sure it's perfectly clear that I only agreed to go to dinner so I could discuss this with him. I've *got* to convince Justin somehow, he's *got* to know that there's nothing between Blair and me, that I'm in love with—" Abruptly, she turned away.

"Oh, rats," Celine said softly, slipping her arm around Lindy's shoulder. "I was afraid of this. I hate seeing you so unhappy."

Lindy set her chin. "It's not over yet. This is one fight I won't back away from. Right now I can't find Justin, and I need Blair's help. But this dinner is strictly business; and Blair had better remember that!"

And though Quadri's glittered with candlelight and crystal, Lindy stuck firmly to her resolve. Obviously sensing that he wasn't going to have much luck at the table, Blair perked up when the small band swung into a number.

"Melinda, would you like to dance?"

"Blair . . ." she warned.

He rose and reached for her hand. "You have some things to discuss with me, don't you? Well, now's your chance."

Swallowing her sharp reply, Lindy headed for the dance floor. He was right behind her, and when she turned, his arm slid familiarly around her waist.

"You're wearing a new dress, aren't you? That sapphire blue is a knockout."

Lindy glanced down at her chiffon cocktail dress. "Thank you. But let's keep this business, shall we?"

"Business? Dancing to Cole Porter? Sacrilege."

"This was your idea, Blair."

"Okay, right. And I'm keeping my word these days. I'm a new man. Did you notice?"

Lindy peered at him critically, perhaps for the first time since he had so unfortunately appeared. The same sardonic wit was constantly with him, but with a new twist; increasingly it was directed at himself. He seemed, she had to admit, a little less belligerent, no longer so sure of his infallibility. His gray eyes had lost some of their arrogance.

"Maybe you have changed, but the difference is probably insignificant."

"Ouch. Well, *you* certainly have changed. I think you've picked up the mean streak I've been trying to lose. . . . Wait, wait. I was only joking. But if you need convincing, this should do it: I'm thinking of taking a real job with the family conglomerate—with responsibility and everything. I've already told the gang to count me out of the new season."

Lindy arched an eyebrow. He'd say anything to score

a point. Still, there was a faint note of sincerity in his tone. Maybe he *was* reforming. Maybe she *could* trust him to explain to Justin.

Justin. At the thought of him, an anxious pain seared her. It was he she should be dancing with. His arms should be around her, his mellow voice whispering to her. She nearly groaned as the weight of her need for him crashed down on her.

Surprisingly, Blair picked up on the fact that her thoughts were elsewhere.

"Come, come, Miss Thorne," he chided softly. "Since, despite my efforts, pleasure seems far from your mind, let's talk business. Now what exactly do you want me to do?"

"You've got to tell ... my friend ... that I didn't invite you here; that I didn't fall willingly into your arms——"

"What a blow to my ego!"

"——that it was all a mistake and there's nothing left between us."

Blair's eyes hooded, and he smiled almost ruefully. "I suppose that's true enough. 'Just friends,' as the saying goes."

"Will you do it? Will you tell him that?"

For a moment, he regarded her closely, saying nothing.

"Well?" she prodded.

"Yes, I'll do it." His voice, Lindy was gratified to note, was clearer, less scornful.

"Thank you."

"You really ... care about this guy, don't you?"

She glanced up sharply, startled by his complete lack of mockery. "Why ... yes, I do ... very much."

He paused, then seemed to shrug back into his habitual mode. "Lucky devil," he grinned, executing a perfect turn. "I guess I'll have to console myself with the beauties of Venice."

Lindy's relief was enormous. Justin *would* understand. He'd wrap her in his powerful arms and squeeze all the anguish out of her. The thought so cheered her, she smiled generously at Blair, only to see that his eyes had fixed on a distant corner of the room.

Curiously, Lindy followed his gaze. She noticed with surprise that the object of his attention was the Contessa D'Alente, standing in a low-cut, clinging gown.

"Why," Lindy muttered to Blair, "that's—" The words froze in her throat as an achingly familiar figure swept into her line of vision.

"He's here!" she gasped. "Blair, Justin is here. You've got to talk to him now. You've..."

She watched in mounting disbelief as Justin, looking neither right nor left, walked straight to Vittoria. The *contessa*, brushing back a wing of jet hair, smiled up at him intimately and hooked a possessive arm through his. While she introduced him to the group she was with, Justin's face remained politely neutral. But when Vittoria stood on tiptoe to whisper something to him, he smiled, and Lindy's heart twisted.

"Could you at least shuffle your feet?" Blair asked mildly, and Lindy realized she'd stopped moving.

"I...I want to sit down," she whispered. But her legs seemed so heavy and rigid, only Blair's buttressing arm got her back to the table. Celine and Steven were dancing, and for that Lindy was thankful. She didn't want to look at or talk to anyone. She stared unseeingly at the napkin she alternately crumpled and smoothed.

"Here, drink this." Blair handed her a snifter of brandy. She hadn't even heard him order it. "Come on, Melinda. Down the hatch. You're pale as a sheet."

She took a gulp of the fiery liquid and shuddered as its warmth spread through her.

"That's better. Looks like we have a minor complication here. Who is she?"

"Vittoria." Lindy's voice came out a weak croak, and clearing her throat barely eased it. "The Contessa D'Alente."

"Ah, yes," Blair said knowingly. "I thought I recognized her. She went big-game hunting last year and almost bagged Parker Wellington's father. Your brooding Italian must be more loaded than I thought."

Lindy blinked in confusion. "Wh—what?"

"Your friend Justin. Where'd his money come from?"

At the mention of his name, Lindy winced.

"No money, Blair. He's an architect, works for a nonprofit agency, yet."

A blessed numbness was settling over her. Part of it, she knew, was the result of the wine she'd drunk earlier and the brandy she still sipped. And part of it . . . With a strange detachment, Lindy perceived it as a sort of self-induced anesthesia, brought on by nearly unbearable hurt. She dimly recalled the feeling, then she realized it was the same icy stiffness she'd felt the day she'd decided to divorce Blair.

"Did you hear me, Melinda? I said that I don't think you have too much to worry about. Old Vittoria has the subtlety of a hurricane, I hear, and she usually does get what she goes after. But, like I said, she only goes after big game. She dropped Wellington when she found out how gigantic Mrs. W.'s divorce settlement would be. An architect? She'll be out of his life before the night's over."

Lindy shook her head slowly, remembering how the *contessa* had practically slavered over Justin at the charity casino. As for him—he'd certainly wasted no time in finding a replacement for her. Even through the insulation of brandy, Lindy could feel a stab of sorrow and mortification. How could she have been so foolish? She'd built a night of passion into an avowal of undying love. Once again she'd tried to play the game without knowing the rules; once again she was the loser.

But she couldn't have been wrong! a woeful voice inside her insisted. The tenderness in his eyes, the declaration in his kiss—that was real. She could not have—had not—imagined it. And yet, had he ever said, in plain words, "I love you, Lindy?"

It was clear that she'd made a horrible mistake. She bit back her humiliation as Steven and Celine returned to the table.

"Nice little orchestra," Celine said, then wrinkled her brow. "Lindy? Are you——"

"Terrific music," Blair cut in, diverting her attention. "We're having some brandy. Will you join us?"

When the waiter brought fresh drinks, Lindy forced a composed expression and looked up. As she did, the glitter of gold lamé caught her eye. Vittoria and Justin were leaving. And then, to her horror, the *contessa* noticed her, gave a blithe wave, and sailed grandly toward their table.

"Why, good evening, Miss Thrump. Imagine seeing you here. Did you have a good dinner?"

Lindy nodded, not bothering to look at Vittoria. With her heart hammering in her chest, she watched Justin as his eyes settled on her. His face hardened as he almost reluctantly approached the table five paces behind the *contessa*.

"I believe you all know Signor DiPalma." The triumph shown in Vittoria's uptilted chin disgusted Lindy.

"Yes," she answered, hating her voice for sounding so high-pitched and strained. She squared her shoulders, determined to preserve the pitiful shreds of her dignity. "This is my sister and brother-in-law, Mr. and Mrs. Marsh. And this is Blair Talbot. The Contessa D'Alente . . . and Justin DiPalma."

With a steely tautness, Justin shook Blair's hand. "How do you do?"

The sound of his voice, beautiful to Lindy even in its harshest tone, almost undid her resolve. She averted her eyes as Blair spoke.

"Of the Tuscan DiPalmas?"

"Yes," Justin replied curtly.

"I see. By the way, I want to tell you——"

Lindy kicked sharply at his shin under the table. To have him say anything now in front of Vittoria would be a degrading disaster. And from the look of things,

Justin wouldn't even be interested.

There was an awkward gap in the conversation. Blair stepped in smoothly. "I wanted to tell you that the chef here is marvelous. You ought to stay for dinner."

"No, no," the sultry Vittoria said. "We must be going. We have . . . things to do. *Ciao,* everyone."

Lindy was inescapably drawn into one last, longing look at Justin as he slowly moved farther and farther away from her. His image seemed to waver a few moments before her eyes, and then he passed into the night.

- *13* -

THE ENDLESS NIGHT finally grayed into dawn. Lindy had
given up trying to sleep hours before. She sat curled up
on the chaise, gazing sightlessly through the window,
her cheek resting on aqua silk damp from intermittent
tears.

She vaguely remembered Blair supporting her on the
way home last evening and Celine tucking her into bed.
She may even have drifted into minutes of fitful sleep.
But soon the effects of the brandy wore off, and Lindy
felt the full brunt of her desolation.

Her world had gone from a dream-come-true to a
nightmare in two days. Only forty-eight hours ago she
had waltzed into this very room on a cloud, with Justin's
kisses still fresh on her skin and his whispers still soft
in her ear.

"Oh God, Justin! I was so sure..."

...So certain he was different. She'd resisted every
cautioning reaction because he was so compelling, his

magnetism so potent. Once she'd felt the strength of his arms, seen the gold flecks of passion in his green eyes.... But what exactly *had* she seen? A gleam of ardor? If so, it was only an illusion, a reflection of his feeling for this city, a deception of the Venetian light. And she had welcomed it, allowing herself to believe that he could care that fervently for her.

Because she, God help her, was completely in love with him.

No! Lindy told herself fiercely. A hot tear rolled down her cheek, and she flicked it away. It was only too obvious that he didn't share her feelings. He was so clever, pretending that his devotion to his work overshadowed everything except his interest in her. When all the while he was concerned only with a quick conquest—and apparently not all that concerned, since he'd already moved on to Vittoria. He was as bad as Blair.

Worse, she bitterly corrected herself; at least Blair was honest about his need for other women. There were no lies about all-or-nothing affection from Blair.

How could she have been so wrong, she thought for the hundredth time. Even if Justin's words had misled her, was it possible his body had? He had made love to her both tenderly and feverishly, stoking the fires long smoldering in her and kindling new ones, holding himself in check until her desire matched his. Was that a lie too?

Wearily, Lindy looked up. The overcast sky let a dingy light into her room. Even that hurt her swollen eyes. She couldn't think anymore. She'd gone over everything so many times, it was all bleeding together into one meaningless stain.

Rising, she took a deep breath. An insidiously sweet odor assaulted her. The flowers—she'd forgotten all about them. Pursing her lips, Lindy dragged them to the balcony door. She stepped into the morning already sticky with heat, grabbed fistful of the blooms, and threw them into the canal until only the skeletal baskets remained.

"I was stupid. I got burned. It's over." And in another two days she'd be on her way—home? Where was that?

"It doesn't matter," she whispered to herself, watching the dying blossoms bob in the murky water. Deliberately, she turned back into her cooler room.

By noon, Lindy felt well enough to bathe and wash her hair. Still, she declined Celine's and the twins' invitation to go with them to a puppet show. When she promised to order some lunch for herself, Celine didn't press. After a few bites of toast and sips of tea, Lindy crawled back into bed, exhausted, and fell into a restless sleep. She awoke in the late afternoon, her throat raw and her muscles aching.

It was hopeless. The more she tried to sort out what had happened, the more her head throbbed. And when she tried to forget it, to imagine instead going on with her life, taunting flashes of her happiness with Justin interrupted her. It was a double loss; not only was he gone, but he had taken with him that glorious sense of completeness she had experienced for a few brief hours. Once more, Lindy felt splintered, her edges rough and unfinished.

She was beginning to wish she'd gone with Celine. At least she would have been occupied. When a knock sounded, she belted her terry-cloth robe and answered the door almost gratefully.

Blair leaned against the jamb with a languid grin.

"Well, well . . . so you're still among the living."

She grimaced. "Barely. What are you doing here?"

"Melinda dear, you must stop trying to charm me like that. I'm so susceptible these days."

"Oh. I'm—I'm sorry. I guess that was rude."

"You're forgiven. But only if you don't leave me standing out here in the hall any longer. May I come in?"

Lindy glanced away. "I don't think so, Blair."

"You *are* a mass of contradictions these days." He

seemed amused. "Well, would it be against your rather complicated code to come downstairs and at least have some other walls to look at?"

Ignoring his sarcasm, Lindy considered the offer. The air-conditioning had been on all day, and the room did smell stale. Maybe a change of scene would help clear her head. "All right. I'll get dressed."

"Fine. Meet me in the bar downstairs."

When he left, Lindy put on a peach-colored peasant dress and combed her hair. Facing herself in the mirror, she saw the evidence of her sleepless night. The soft shade of her clothes helped a little, but she still thought she looked ghastly. Quickly, she brushed on a bit of makeup.

The bar was nearly deserted at that time of day, and she found Blair easily. He was sipping what looked like a Bloody Mary and smoking a thin cigar.

"Ah, you look much better. Does this prescription interest you?" He tipped his glass to her.

"No, I just want fruit juice."

Summoning the waiter, he gave her order and then turned back toward Lindy.

"So how do you feel?" he asked gently.

She shook her head. "I don't know. Confused. Angry. Numb. Everything happened so fast last night. . . ."

"Hmm, yes. Well, you know the determined *contessa* isn't about to let any grass grow under her dainty little feet. One does not stay queen of the jungle that way."

"No, one does not." She couldn't compete with Vittoria if she wanted to. She lacked the necessary killer instinct.

"Melinda . . ." Blair puffed a moment on his cigar. "I don't know if this will make you feel better or worse, but it might explain something. I told you the dear *contessa* is damned near unstoppable when she sets her sights. Well, it now appears that your friend Justin must have been her target all along."

The waiter brought her juice, and Lindy toyed with the glass, frowning.

"What do you mean?"

"Apparently he never saw fit to mention it to you, but the DiPalma family has one of the finest vineyards in Tuscany. You've probably even drunk some of their wine. They bottle under the label of *Nettare di Vita*—Nectar of Life. Aptly named, in my opinion. Anyway, unless he's been disowned for some disastrous reason, your Justin DiPalma is most likely a very wealthy man."

Lindy stared at him, stunned. Justin had never even given her a clue. She thought back to the day they'd spent on the sailboat, when he'd spoken about his background. There had been nothing to suggest any riches. True, his clothes were beautifully tailored and his Bulgari watch obviously expensive. But they were the trappings of success, not necessarily wealth.

Could he have been, as Blair said, disowned, and now didn't care to discuss it? No, his father had been the rebel, not Justin. She remembered the affection in his tone when he talked about his *nonno*. And as she recalled his voice that day, images of him came with it—the sunlight gleaming blue black in his hair and golden bronze on his skin, the hunger deepening his eyes as he lay beside her on the beach, the salty tang of his lips and the sleek caress of his body . . .

She braced against the bittersweet pain. All that was history now. The man she thought she knew so well was simply another illusion.

Blair squeezed her arm.

"If it's any comfort, the odds were stacked as soon as Vittoria decided to go after him. She's so persistent when she's on a chase, she hardly ever comes out empty-handed."

"Maybe so." Compressing her lips, Lindy gazed fixedly at her glass. "But you saw him last night. Nobody was twisting his arm."

"Well, my dear, listen to the voice of too much experience. Sometimes it's easy to fall prey to a woman like the *contessa*. The tragedy of it is that you wake up one morning and find she's dumped you before you could dump her. Then you think of the perfectly terrific person you threw over for her in the first place. You feel very sorry and want to kick yourself for being so dumb, for making such a stupid mistake. Know what I mean?"

Startled, Lindy studied Blair. His smile was ironic, but there was a melancholy cast to his gray eyes. When she didn't speak after a few moments of peering at him, his eyes hooded over and matched the shade of his grin.

"I told you it was the voice of experience. You know, Melinda, I've missed you."

She sniffed skeptically. "Come on, Blair. There were dozens of women trailing after you when we were married. I can picture the rush when we got divorced. Must have looked like a sale day at Bloomingdale's."

He marked an imaginary point for her side in the air.

"Good one. Now, I'm not saying I have anything against beautiful women chasing after me—*au contraire*. But sooner or later, you have to talk to these birds of paradise. It's always such a disappointment to realize that they have fried mush for brains."

"Did you ever stop to think," Lindy said dryly, "that you're prowling in the wrong jungle? There are some intelligent women out there; you just have to look in the right places. I suppose that's never occurred to you, though."

"What has occurred to me," he answered, "is that we had a hell of a lot of fun together, you and I."

"Sure we did. You're an expert at playing. It's a fine art with you. Then, when the fun gets too predictable, you do something outrageous to stir up a nice juicy fight."

"Exactly. And when that gets tedious, we patch things up and have fun again. Life is never boring that way."

Lindy knew he meant it. Blair didn't care very much about anything, so he had to get his stimulation from external sources. On the other hand, she reminded herself, that made him one of the least vulnerable people she'd ever met. He would never have to feel the dreadful hurt she had experienced lately. There *was* something to be said for his style after all.

"Listen," he said, draining his drink and signaling for another, "will you do me one favor? I mean, in light of the fact that I did you a favor and practically carried you home last night?"

"How gallant of you to bring it up."

"All right, all right. I merely want to point out that you owe me one because I think your first instinct here is going to be a flat refusal. I want you to hear me out, okay?"

"Okay . . . I guess."

"I want you to think about seeing me again. I—"

"No."

"Melinda, you promised to listen."

"Blair, we don't look at things the same way."

"Correction: Past tense. We didn't used to. I freely admit, I was scared off by your creeping domesticity. I guess I *am* a jungle animal. But there's nothing wrong with that, is there? After all, God made lions as well as house cats. . . . Anyway, these days it seems that I'm getting a little tamer and you're suddenly showing some of the old tiger spirit. And I'll tell you quite frankly, it's a definite turn-on."

"Blair, we would fight from dawn to dusk, and you know it."

"Maybe." His smile had a spark of eroticism. "But after dark we'd *really* have fun, and if your memory is intact, my dear, *you* know *that!*"

Annoyed, Lindy shook her head. "You are incorrigible."

Blair leaned forward and covered her hand with his.

"You know what I'm saying is true. And now that the stardust is gone, now that we understand each other better and know what to expect . . . Don't you see what fun we could have? *No* strings, Melinda—for either of us. You'd be free to come and go as you like. We could——"

Pulling away, Lindy stood up suddenly. "Don't get the wrong idea, Blair. This meeting you, this was being polite, getting out for a minute. This was not a change of heart. I'm going for a walk. Good-bye."

"Melinda——"

She swept past his outstretched arm, hurrying through the bar and outside onto the *riva*. The heat assailed her, and she sucked in a heavy breath. Where to? She couldn't face St. Mark's Square or any of the other places she'd been to with Justin. His absence now would only emphasize her loneliness. Turning in the opposite direction, she saw a *vaporetto* chugging toward the quay. Quickening her steps, fishing in her purse for the fare, Lindy reached the dock just as the water-bus pulled alongside. It never really stopped, but as it slowed for ten seconds or so, passengers jumped on or off, and she followed their example.

The *vaporetto* was crowded, but she found a seat toward the rear and sank onto it as the boat moved into the Basin of St. Mark. They picked up speed, stirring a reluctant breeze. Lindy lifted her face to it gratefully.

It felt good to be moving without any effort of her own, chasing away the mental cobwebs Blair had created. He was still very good at that. Her mouth set in irritation. He seemed to delight in taking her by surprise with one of his bold and presumptuous gestures. First the kiss in the lobby and now this preposterous suggestion of his—it was nothing more than a blatant proposition. Only Blair would have the gall to bring it up, and then to sneak in that sly reminder of their pleasure in the bedroom! He was completely maddening. And he knew exactly how to get to her.

Leaning on the rail, Lindy stared out over the water. While they had been married, she'd thought their love life was good. Now she knew better. Blair was very much attuned to his own needs, very little to hers. And the reason she realized this was . . .

She rested her chin on her fist as the sadness rolled over her once more. Could she ever bear another man's touch after knowing the sweetness of Justin's? After lying in his arms, feeling his heart pounding in counterpoint to hers, floating dizzily with him on higher planes than she ever dreamed possible? After being bound so closely to him that she knew his soul as well as her own?...

But she didn't, she remembered miserably. She didn't know him at all.

The *vaporetto* slowed as it approached land. The captain called "Zecca!" for the island of Giudecca, and a few other phrases Lindy didn't understand. After trading a couple of passengers, they were on their way again. Lindy tried to tug her thoughts away from Justin, but even now, his magnetism was powerful, if only as a tormenting reminder of what she had lost...and what Vittoria had gained.

But she really shouldn't be so shocked, Lindy thought. It was obvious now that the *contessa* was more his type anyway.

Shifting in her seat, beginning to feel restless, Lindy looked over to her left as the water-bus angled away from Giudecca. She let her gaze wander over the island's waterfront, hoping to distract herself with the scenery. But everything looked dull and listless. The sun still skulked behind stodgy gray clouds. Without its powdery pastel light, the *palazzi* and churches seemed almost shabby.

A large building loomed in her sight, and with a sharp pang, she recognized the Church of the Redeemer. Suddenly the *vaporetto* felt confining.

She turned to the elderly man sitting beside her and asked, "When is the next stop?"

He shrugged. *"Non capisc', signorina."*

She stood up, balancing as the boat chopped through the canal, searching the shoreline for the next dock. It seemed like ages before the captain shouted, *"Zattere al Gesuati!"*

She debarked in the midst of the other passengers and stood a moment in front of the triple-domed church of the *Gesuati*. It was an unfamiliar area. Lindy decided to stay on the *fondamente*, the wide path along the canal.

She started walking and nearly stumbled when it dawned on her what the *vaporetto* captain had said. Zattere — where she and Justin were supposed to go for a stroll that fateful evening, where he had wanted to show her the building he was working on.

She shuffled to a stop, glancing nervously around her. Could he be here even now? He'd said the restoration was of a big, mustard-colored building. She slowly resumed her pace, half dreading, half hoping she'd see it. And as she peered ahead she noticed that farther down a portion of the sidewalk was roped off. With a pulse-pounding certainty, Lindy knew that was the place.

She hesitated. An alley jutting to the left offered her a convenient escape, but she strode right past it, as if pulled forward. Closer and closer she drew until the building appeared in her oblique line of vision, confirming what she already knew. Its dark yellow facade bore a network of scaffolding, and even now workmen, barechested against the heat, chipped at the flaking surface.

Pausing, Lindy watched their limited progress. This was Justin's passion at the moment, this construction of mortar and marble. She had no doubt that under his loving hands it would be transformed into something better than it had ever been before — not unlike she herself had been, if only briefly.

As she gazed thoughtfully at the former warehouse, the door opened and another worker appeared. He called over his shoulder to the man who followed him onto the Zattere.

Lindy's heart vaulted in her chest. It was Justin, in rolled-up shirt-sleeves, opening a blueprint and motioning while the worker listened. She sidled through a sparse crowd to stand under the awning of a shop three doors away, where she could watch less conspicuously. She didn't want to be discovered; she only wanted to look at him a while.

Justin's brow knit in concentration as he studied the plan and explained it to the foreman. Finally, the worker nodded, and Justin clapped him on the back, grinning.

Lindy caught her breath. His smile was so dazzlingly familiar.

With the rewound blueprint under one arm, he paced up and down before the building, calling directions, trading ripostes with the men. At one point he seemed to want a better look, and he hoisted himself up on the scaffolding. His muscles strained against his shirt. Lindy couldn't take her eyes away from him.

As he jumped down and dusted off his hands, he scanned the sky and water, apparently searching for clues to the weather. And as his gaze fanned across the Zattere, he suddenly tensed. Lindy realized he was looking right at her.

She froze. He recovered first, coming slowly toward her. She was torn between bolting away and running to embrace him. Instead, she did nothing.

He had to duck under the awning.

"Hello." The word sounded forced. Polite, but far from cordial.

"Hi," Lindy answered. She cast her eyes downward, afraid that her hurt and longing and, yes, love, lay naked in them.

"Are you . . . shopping?"

Setting a guard around herself, Lindy looked up.

"Umm, yes. Shopping . . . for gifts and things."

Justin nodded. A muscle in his jaw twitched.

"Blair with you?"

She shook her head quickly. "No. He's back at the hotel."

Justin's eyes thunderclouded before he turned to his building.

"I've got to get to work," he said stiffly. "Good-bye." His back hunched against her as he stalked away.

No! Wait! Lindy wanted to cry—You don't understand. She clenched her teeth. Damn her unfortunate choice of words! Justin probably thought she and Blair were sharing her room by now.

For one wild moment, she almost ran after him, to throw herself into his arms and let her love spill out. If only he'd looked back, made one relenting gesture, anything to tell her there was a chance of regaining their closeness. . . .

But he didn't. And Lindy couldn't risk the mortification of his rejecting her outright. Deliberately, she spun and headed back to the water-bus stop, with her composure no more than a fragile shell around her.

She didn't know how long she waited, and she didn't notice the sky changing until she heard a rumble and, glancing up, saw it was an angry pewter. The *vaporetto* lumbered up to the dock, and she climbed aboard. The other, more canny passengers, anticipating the rain, claimed the seats on the less exposed left side and middle. Lindy took a seat on the open side, wishing that the quickened wind would whip all the confusion and regret out of her.

But despite her muddled thoughts, one thing seemed clear: No matter how much she yearned for Justin, for the shelter of his arms and the exhilaration of his kiss, it was not meant to be. The question was, why had he been attracted to her in the first place? Was it just the challenge of conquest?

She frowned in concentration, really needing to understand. It didn't seem logical, even conceding that Justin was not the man she thought she knew. He was challenged enough by his work, by the sometimes impossible task of preserving buildings that wanted only to crumble into the lagoon. Daring and defiance were in his nature. He didn't need to create them the way that Blair did.

So why had Justin pursued her? There was only one answer, and Lindy reluctantly had to face it. His passion from the beginning had been his work with *Bell'Italia*. Wasn't it logical that he'd do anything—*anything*—to confirm his dedication to the architecture of old *Venezia*? Including making love to the sister-in-law of a man whose support he wanted.

She closed her eyes against the stinging wind. She suddenly didn't want to see this city that had somehow become her rival now. For she knew that neither Vittoria nor Madame Delphine nor any other woman meant any more to Justin than she had. Venice was his very jealous mistress, and her beauty an illusion that he seemed determined to foster. She couldn't fight that.

As the water-bus cut its speed for the stop on the Giudecca, it rocked in water that was starting to churn. The warning thunder sounded closer, and Lindy felt the lash of the wind. She was suddenly anxious to get back to the hotel. She found herself counting ahead to the hour she would be leaving this place, wondering where she would go, what she would do. She absolutely did not want to mope and ache for what might have been.

She wondered where Blair was going next.

It was true; they did have fun. He kept every gathering lively with his wit, even when it was needle sharp. Maybe she should give some thought to his proposition. At least he was honest about it. No declarations of love and devotion, just a purely sensual experience with a familiar old flame. Light and casual. It surely couldn't hurt her any more than falling deeply in love had.

Just as they approached her stop, the sky opened up in a weeping rage. Lindy jumped ashore, bent her head, and started running toward the Danieli. The battering rain soaked her before she'd gone ten feet, coldly plastering her cotton dress to her body.

Finally, with much relief, she entered the lobby. As she passed the desk, she hesitated and the clerk looked up questioningly.

"Is a Mr. Blair Talbot registered here?"

"One moment, Signorina Thorne... Ah, yes. He's in room——"

"Thank you, I just wanted to know if he's still here."

There was plenty of time to talk to him. Right now, more than anything, she needed a long, hot bath to soothe away the chill she felt, both inside and out.

· 14 ·

"HERE'S TO OUR last night in Venice," Steven said, raising his liqueur glass. "A lovely city, steeped in history. Children, I hope you learned a lot..."

Celine leaned toward her sister. "He's always like this at the end of a project. Talks and talks. Are you all right? You didn't eat much."

"I'm fine," Lindy insisted. But she was secretly grateful when Steven claimed his wife's attention.

She glanced distractedly around the group gathered at Florian's, enjoying their after-dinner drinks amid the turn-of-the-century decor. The purpose of the affair, sponsored by *Patria Grande,* was to announce the results of the studies Steven and the other experts had made. From the self-satisfied grins on many of the faces, Lindy surmised that a strong case for modernization had been built.

"More?"

Blinking, Lindy saw Blair, sitting at her right, holding up a squat bottle by its thin neck. "Wh—what?"

"More Amaretto?" he asked. When she nodded, he tipped it to her glass. "Did you know that Amaretto is supposed to be the drink of lovers?"

She sipped the mildly bitter liqueur. How appropriate, she thought glumly. Love certainly hadn't been sweet for her. A heaviness centered in her chest. It hadn't been the easiest day. . . .

She'd spent most of it listlessly packing. And staring through the window. The squall had blown itself out shortly after midnight, and the new day sparkled with rain-freshened air. Lindy had barely noticed it. Her vision was still gloomily colored with the memory of Justin's chiseled scowl.

Celine kept popping in and out of her room with meaningless questions and worried looks. Finally, late in the afternoon, she cornered Lindy with a pot of coffee.

"Exactly what is going on about Justin? Is there any chance . . . ?"

Mutely, Lindy signalled No. It was decisive. Final. Swallowing her misery, she told Celine in a bleak monotone about seeing him on the Zattere.

"You were right, Celine," she whispered at the end. "It was just a silly summer romance. And worst of all . . . worst of all . . ." Her pride nearly caught in her throat. "I think he was only using me to get to Steven. Venice is all he cares for. I think he just wanted the important American consultant on his side."

"The nerve of him!" Celine's foot tapped her indignance. "Well, I'm just going to speak to Steven about that." Wasting no time, she marched over to their room, dragged him back, and repeated Lindy's theory.

"He certainly didn't strike me as the devious type," Steven commented when he'd heard it.

Lindy laughed without a hint of mirth. "Me neither, but then it seems we didn't know the half of him." Briefly, trying not to sound as disgruntled as she felt, she told him about the DiPalma vineyards and the games with Vittoria. "So he has his money, and it now appears that the dear *contessa* has him. They both should be supremely happy." She spun around so he wouldn't see her traitorous tears.

Steven cleared his throat, obviously uncomfortable with her mood. "Well, I wouldn't know about that, Lindy, but I don't think DiPalma is very happy these days."

Frowning, Lindy brushed the wetness from her cheeks and faced her brother-in-law.

"What do you mean?"

"It looks like he hasn't got a chance of saving the D'Alente home. Foundation's terribly weak; a hazzard, really. Apparently, it will be one of the first buildings razed. But the countess is getting paid a tidy sum for it, and that should please her. Those places cost plenty to keep up, and she'd been borrowing against it for years."

Lindy pondered a moment, then stared up at him.

"Steven, do you mean to tell me that the *contessa* is broke?"

"Yes, I believe that is accurate."

"Then when," she continued thoughtfully, "was the decision made to buy her house and tear it down?"

"Just today. The reports were in long ago, but the decision was made only today."

Interesting . . . but what did it all mean?

Think like a Venetian, Lindy told herself. That was the key—to tear away the filmy layers one by one, to see through the mirage to the well-concealed truth.

So Vittoria's fortune had been made the day after she turned up in public with Justin displayed like a hunting trophy. Was that a coincidence? Maybe . . . and maybe the real prize was having her home declared a disaster. That was Byzantine enough, Lindy mused grimly; that fit the ambience of Venice. And just who was in the position to bestow that prize?

"Gilberti," Lindy breathed.

Steven, adjusting his glasses, looked up.

"Huh? Oh, yes. It was Gilberti; he cast the deciding vote."

Of course! Vittoria was the decoy, to lure Justin away from Lindy and the real prey, Steven. Gilberti didn't want even the slightest *Bell'Italia* influence on the American consultant. And when Vittoria delivered, when she snared Justin, Gilberti rewarded her with his vote. Lindy could imagine how eagerly the *contessa* went along with the scheme, having nothing to lose and both a fortune and a rich, handsome prospective husband to gain. No wonder Vittoria was so determined. And who could blame Justin for falling into her clutches?

Lindy could.

After she'd understood all that, her anger had propelled her through the rest of her packing. It was galling to think she'd been little more than a pawn to those people. Setting her mouth sternly, she vowed never again to get involved with intrigue. No more idealistic lost causes, and no more torrid summer romances. There was just too much danger of devastation in any kind of passion.

Throughout the long afternoon, she paced restlessly, anxious to leave Venice, wishing their flight left sooner than tomorrow morning. All her clothes were folded in their suitcases, each piece she'd worn with Justin tucked in with a poignant memory. She fretted about what to wear to the dinner, finally settling on the off-shouldered white dress she'd worn to the charity casino. She had no choice. Her only other option was the gown she'd had on the night of *Redentore*. She feared she could never touch that dress again without a stab of regret.

It was probably better that way, she reminded herself.

She might have been convinced, but then she glanced around her room for any stray belongings and found one gleaming sweetly from the top of the bureau.

The glass sailboat Justin had given her. Lindy grasped it gently and with loving fingertips caressed each smooth line. Holding it up to the window, she watched the dying sunlight glisten through it, changing from emerald to aquamarine to sapphire. Then, borrowing some tissue paper from her ball gown, she wrapped the sailboat ever so carefully and found a sheltered place for it in the suitcase. It would be the one beautiful thing she'd salvage from this disastrous trip.

If she could just make it through this evening, she had promised herself, she'd be able to stand it. . . .

"Melinda?"

With a start, she jerked back to the present.

"Melinda, dear," Blair said mildly, "you can't keep drifting off to another planet like that. Who will laugh at my jokes?"

"We will, Uncle Blair!" Tammy piped up.

Todd gave her a disgusted look. "We aren't s'posed to call him uncle any more, dummy."

"Todd," Celine warned. "No name-calling."

"But she said——"

"I know. Maybe we should go wash your hands. Come on."

Ignoring their protests, she swept them both out of the room. Blair chuckled softly.

"You know what they say . . . 'Out of the mouths of babes.' Maybe it's a sign. What do you think?"

Lindy ducked her head. "I don't know. You promised you wouldn't——"

"—pressure you. Right." Leaning forward, he lit one of his pencil-thin cigars and smiled lazily. "But I'm not above shamelessly tempting you. Listen to this: Tomorrow I'm renting a car and driving down the coast to Rimini. Guy and Mimi will be anchoring there in a few days, and then they're off to cruise the Greek Isles for a month. I'm invited, along with a guest of my choice. How's that for an offer you can't refuse?"

It did sound lovely. Guy and Mimi were quieter than most of Blair's friends, and less flamboyant. Four weeks of sun to cauterize her wounds . . .

"It *is* tempting, Blair. Let me think about it."

Nodding affably, he blew out a curtain of smoke. As it lifted, Lindy felt her mouth go dry. Across the room, a late-coming couple was being seated—Vittoria in a dress of triumphant red, and beside her, directly opposite Lindy, Justin.

As soon as he took his chair, he scanned the room until his gaze locked on her. She caught her breath. His expression was somewhere between anger and disbelief, though Lindy couldn't be sure if she was the cause of it. It just as easily—and more probably—could have been due to the news that another *palazzo* was coming down.

But she didn't care. She almost welcomed the intensity in his eyes, the strength of his firm jaw . . . It set her heart racing so that she felt the surge of her blood from her fingertips to her toes. When at last he broke the contact and looked away, Lindy leaned back in her chair, enervated, groaning internally. When, oh when, would she stop reacting so severely to the sight of him?

The speeches were beginning. Since the group was small, no microphones were needed. An elegant man stood and spoke in Italian, with the interpretor translating phrase for phrase beside him, introducing Ugo Gilberti. He rose to enthusiastic approval, rocking back and forth on his heels as he spoke.

"*Signore e signori* . . . Ladies and gentlemen . . ." Gilberti beamed. "I think in honor of our guests from America, tonight I speak English."

The translator obligingly switched to Italian. Gilberti brought an easel forward and dramatically revealed a rendering of a crack-faced *palazzo*.

"This is the first step for *Il Rinnovo,* the renewal of *Venezia.*" He waited for the smattering of applause to wear out. "La Contessa D'Alente has given us our number-one project. Her family home, sad to say, is unsafe. Cracks. Leaks. Three, maybe four houses in this area are the same. We remove danger and . . . *ècco!*—behold!"

He displayed the next drawing, a glass office building rising out of the lagoon and looking, Lindy thought, like a giant gridded ice cube.

"He's kidding," she murmured to Steven. "He's got to be kidding."

Steven shrugged and shook his head. "I don't think so, Lindy. Actually, it shows an efficient use of space and cost."

She sniffed. "Looks ridiculous."

A little out of breath, Celine slipped back into her seat. "Did I miss much?"

"What took you so long?" Lindy whispered as Gilberti resumed his speech. "And where are the kids?"

"They were getting restless. I sent for the hotel launch and the babysitter. Which reminds me . . ." She reached into her handbag for a large envelope. "I just found this in my purse when I tipped the launch captain. It came today while you were in the tub, and in the confusion of packing, I forgot all about it. I'm really sorry. I paid the boy who delivered it, so don't worry——"

Impatiently, Lindy tore open the envelope, and a cardboard folder tumbled out. Heat flushed her cheeks and exploded at her temples.

It was the photograph the young boy had taken the night of *Redentore*. There she was in the gondola, wrapped in Justin's embrace, her head nestled on his shoulder. A radiant expression of joy, spiced with eagerness, lit the face in the picture. And when she noticed Justin's eyes, already warm with desire, she remembered why.

Quickly, before anyone should want to see it, Lindy turned the photo over on the table. Incredibly, that brief visual reminder had given her total recall of the feeling she'd had at that very instant. Such a vivid, exalted feeling.

Such thrilling, absolute love.

"Lindy?"

She waved Celine off and took a gulp of the liqueur

that was supposed to be sipped. It made her eyes water, but it also jolted her out of her lethargy. It was crazy, she thought desperately, crazy to deny feelings of pain and loss. It only made them more unbearable. For such a very long time she had berated herself for reacting so strongly to things that were important to her. Whether the matter at hand was the love of a passionate man or the glory of a magnificent city, it was good to get involved, she realized with growing conviction. Unless you were willing to lay your beliefs on the line, they weren't worth a damn.

"Venezia is a great city," Gilberti was saying proudly. And Lindy knew then that it was. Because greatness did not mean perfection, but it did mean rising above the flaws and concentrating on the beauty.

"This," Gilberti fairly shouted, pointing to the proposed building, "is the future of *Venezia!"*

"No, it isn't."

There was a stunned silence, and Lindy realized she'd spoken aloud—and that the small gathering had heard her clearly. Her cheeks flamed, but she tilted her chin up defiantly.

"Scusi, signorina," Gilberti said smugly. "If you wish to speak, we are happy for comments." A few of his compatriots chuckled at his thinly veiled sarcasm, which obviously was intended to put her in her place.

Lindy's temper was flaring, but for once she didn't blow up. Instead, she used the force of her anger to fuel her resolve. Outwardly calm, she stood.

"Thank you, Signor Gilberti," she said in measured tones. "I do wish to speak."

"Lindy..." Celine murmured. Lindy silenced her with a brisk wave.

"I know there are parts of this city that cannot survive. Places where the damages of time and neglect cannot be reversed. For the good of the city and the safety of her people, those places must be demolished. It's sad, but I realize it must be done."

She paused to give the translator a chance to catch up, unaware of the fire that was beginning to leap in her eyes.

"So cut out the diseased parts if you must. But for the love of God, don't replace them with monstrosities like that!"

She flicked her hand disdainfully at the easel. Gilberti turned florid, and there were mutterings of protest from the audience. Lindy didn't care. Her indignation seemed to energize her.

"Would you replace a missing arm with an iron bar, just because it was fast and cheap?" she demanded. "Of course not. Yet that's what you'll be doing to this city if you insist on something like that. At least have some respect for the dignity of Venice. Design something that suits her soul."

The mumblings were becoming louder, and Gilberti mopped his ample brow. Lindy knew she wouldn't have much time left, so she went on quickly.

"I know you think that I'm an outsider, that I have no business saying anything, that the fate of Venice ultimately will be decided by her own people. But let me tell you this."

The fire spread to her heart, and her words were seared with emotion. "Your ancestors and your children . . . and your children's children will not thank you for destroying the beauty, the glory, the very heart and greatness of *Venezia*. You owe it to all of them to preserve as much as you can. Think about it! It's all there, in every cobblestone, in every brushstroke on a mural, in every roof and doorway. Venetians made those things; they cared deeply for them—and only Venetians can save them."

The translator raced through the Italian, and when he finished, the entire room was silent. Even the imperturbable waiters stood stock-still.

Lindy's chest was heaving. The fire had run its course. "That's all I have to say," she murmured, spinning and hurrying out of the restaurant.

She ran out to the magnificent St. Mark's Square,

with its glorious masterpiece of a cathedral, floodlit against the dark night. Lindy found an empty table just outside Florian's and sat down with a deep sigh. She felt drained, yet oddly refreshed, as if a milestone had been passed and she was ready for a new journey.

A hand clasped her shoulder.

"Brava," Blair murmured. "What a speech. I knew we were two of a kind." Sitting, he grinned at her. "And there are so few of us connoisseurs of decadence left. You really told them. And with such style!"

Lightly, almost idly, he stroked her forearm. "We are going to have some great times. You're just what I need to liven up my life."

Blair was still smiling, but Lindy noticed that there was no anticipation, no real emotion of any sort in his gray eyes. He might have changed, but she at last realized that he had just altered a small, outward part of himself. He was still attuned to his own distorted perceptions and jaded needs. And with sudden, blinding insight, Lindy knew that she could never be happy with a man who had no dreams.

Gently, but firmly, she removed his hand from her arm.

"Blair . . . It's not going to work. I—I need a relationship that promises more than lots of fun. Do you know what I mean?"

He sat back, measuring her through hooded eyes.

"I guess I do."

His mouth curved wryly. "What if I threw in the Greek Isles *and* the South Seas?" When she shook her head, he sighed. "My bad luck. The lady's beyond a bribe. Well, with stakes like that, I guess I won't be lonely long."

Lindy knew he was right. There were enough pleasure-seeking jetsetters to see to that.

"I wish you well, Blair."

"Thanks. I think you really do." He stood, lighting another cigar with a flourish. Lindy detected a tinge of regret in his smile.

"Be happy, Melinda." He touched her cheek once and was gone.

It was as if another burden had lifted. Blair's cynicism had always darkened her spirit. She felt better than she had in days.

"May I sit for just a moment?"

Lindy looked up and her heart lurched madly. Justin towered beside her, silhouetted in the light reflected from the piazza.

Somehow she found her voice. "Y—Yes. Please do."

He lowered himself into the cafe chair, and for a breathless moment neither of them spoke. Lindy had all she could do to keep from staring. His vitality still captivated her. With a pang, she realized that for the rest of her life, no other man would strike this vibrant a chord in her.

"I just wanted to tell you," he began, "that you were wonderful in there."

She flushed, unsure how to respond. His face, smooth and luminously handsome in the play of light and shadow, showed his tight control. Lindy wished she dared to look into his eyes.

"I probably should have kept my mouth shut," she murmured, "but I just couldn't stand it. What they wanted to do was criminal."

Justin smiled briefly. "Thank God there are still a few of us left who think so. I feel that same outrage, that same horror. But so often I end up walking away, silent and furious, afraid I'll explode. Believe me, *Bell'Italia* could use your eloquence." His expression softened, strangely stirring Lindy. "I'd ask them to offer you a job if you were . . . staying. . . ."

As his voice trailed off, Lindy found the courage to meet his gaze. The glow in his eyes nearly burned through her. No, she told herself firmly, glancing away. Whatever had been between them was over. But why didn't that message get through to her trembling hands?

From the corner of her eye, she saw Justin's chest rise and fall in a deep breath. When he spoke, the tautness had returned. "Well, I won't keep you. But I wanted to tell you that I appreciate what you did. Oh, yes, and you might be interested in this—the Palazzo D'Alente was sabotaged."

"What!"

"Yes. It was made to look more decayed than it was so that all the buildings around it apparently would have to come down too."

"How did you find out?"

Justin flashed a wry smile. "A certain ambitious *contessa* was too sure of me. She rather smugly divulged the whole sordid plot. But it was old news. I had done my own quiet little study when I first heard her house might be razed."

Lindy blinked in amazement. "Then you weren't . . . I mean, you and Vittoria aren't . . ."

"No. And we never were." His mouth was serious. He rested one of his hands on the table, drumming his long, beautiful fingers.

"I just had to follow my hunch, to see what she was up to. And well . . . I didn't want to interfere if you were going to try again with your ex-husband."

An uncomfortable silence stretched between them. Desperately, Lindy searched for a way to explain, to make sense of the whole hideous mess. But she couldn't find a place to begin, knowing it would end with a feverish declaration of her love. . . . Yes, her everlasting, undying love for him. And she would not, could not bear another crushing rejection. There were still too many unanswered questions.

Justin started to rise, and Lindy grasped his arm for a short, electric second. "Wait!" she blurted. "Why weren't you honest with me? I thought I knew you, especially after the way we talked—" She flushed, remembering that at the time they had been naked beneath his sheets, drowsy with sated desire.

Her eyes downcast, Lindy agitatedly rubbed a circle on the tabletop. "You never told me about the Tuscan DiPalmas—the vineyards, the family fortune."

"Only because it's not important to me. What do you think I am—a playboy dabbling in romantic causes? I happen to care intensely for the things I believe in. Don't you know that?"

She glanced quickly at him. The ardent power of his gaze jolted her, and she wondered why she had ever doubted him. From the moment she'd set eyes on him, a bare two weeks ago in this very square, she'd known with a soul-deep certainty that this was a fiercely passionate man, a man incapable of shallow deception, who would give total, uncompromising love...

But would he want to give it to her?

The answer was so acutely important to Lindy, she just couldn't risk finding out. Her throat constricted and she blinked furiously to avoid the threatening rush of tears.

"I won't bother you anymore, Lindy."

She realized he was standing, but she couldn't raise her head, not with her eyes so dangerously full.

"Arrivederci...I hope you'll...always be happy."

Swallowing the sob that rose in her, Lindy looked up. His tall, muscular form was blending into the crowd.

"Justin..." she whispered feebly, but she could not move, could only sit there as his image grew smaller in the distance.

And then her pain gave way to panic as it dawned on her that the man she loved was walking out of her life. All because she was too proud, too afraid to fight for him. She who had put herself on the line for a woman in New York she barely knew and a city she'd only visited. Everything she'd said in defense of Venice was magnified in her love for Justin. And only she could preserve *that* treasure.

She jumped up so fast her chair tumbled over behind her. Mindlessly she ran through the crowd, frantically calling his name, her eyes picking up and never leaving that broad back.

Gradually, she gained on him. When she was a scarce

twenty yards away, he suddenly stopped, planted his feet determinedly, and whirled toward her.

"Lindy!" He raced to her and swept her up in his powerful arms, his green eyes blazing. "I can't let you go. I love you, Lindy. I have to have you. And by God, I'll fight with my last ounce of strength for you. Do you understand me? I love you!"

His demanding lips pressed hers, sweetly draining all her doubts and fears. Joy rose from her heart, and all Lindy could do was let it flow. At last she tilted her head back. "Oh, darling, I was so stupid..."

"No more than I, *cara*. But now we know." His face shone inches from hers, a beacon of love. *"Amore mia*, you are the wonder of my life. It's taken me so long to admit it to myself...but my life, all that I believe in, is meaningless without you, Lindy. We belong together."

"Yes...oh, yes."

They shared a smile—a silent pact that was a promise. With his arm around her shoulder and hers around his waist, they walked slowly across the square, under the velvet Venetian sky.

Second Chance at Love™

Please turn
the page
for our questionnaire
and an exciting

SECOND CHANCE

AT LOVE
offer!!!

QUESTIONNAIRE

1. How many romances do you buy each month
   - ☐ 5 or less
   - ☐ 5 to 10
   - ☐ more than 10

2. Do you like, primarily
   - ☐ modern-day romances
   - ☐ Regency period romances
   - ☐ both, equally
   - ☐ other historical romances

3. Were the love scenes in this novel
   - ☐ too explicit
   - ☐ not explicit enough
   - ☐ handled tastefully

4. Do you prefer stories set
   - ☐ in the USA
   - ☐ in foreign countries
   - ☐ both, equally

5. How old do you like your heroines to be
   - ☐ 17 to 22
   - ☐ 23 to 27
   - ☐ 28 to 32
   - ☐ 33 to 40
   - ☐ over 40

6. The length of this book is
   - ☐ too short
   - ☐ just right
   - ☐ too long

7. The main reason I buy a romance is
   - ☐ a friend's recommendation
   - ☐ a bookseller's recommendation
   - ☐ because of the cover
   - ☐ other reason:_____

8. Where did you buy this book?
   - ☐ chain store (drug, department, etc.)
   - ☐ bookstore
   - ☐ supermarket
   - ☐ other:_____

9. Mind telling your age?
   Our lips are sealed…
   - ☐ under 18
   - ☐ 18 to 30
   - ☐ 31 to 45
   - ☐ over 45

10. Check here if you would like to
    - ☐ receive the SECOND CHANCE AT LOVE Newsletter

. . . .

Fill-in your name and address below:

name:_____

street address:_____

city_____ state_____ zip_____

Please share your other ideas about romances with us on an additional sheet and attach it securely to this questionnaire.

PLEASE RETURN THIS QUESTIONNAIRE TO:
SECOND CHANCE AT LOVE, THE BERKLEY/JOVE PUBLISHING GROUP
200 Madison Avenue, New York, New York 10016

Dear Reader,

Welcome to the <u>Second Chance at Love</u> circle of readers! The <u>Second Chance at Love</u> romances are written with *you* in mind. To find out more about you and what you like, we'd like to ask you to take a few moments and fill out the questionnaire on the opposite page and return it to us. And, in return, we'll pay for postage on the Second Chance order you place using the coupon that follows.

_____ 05703-7 **FLAMENCO NIGHTS** #1 Susanna Collins

_____ 05637-5 **WINTER LOVE SONG** #2
Meredith Kingston

_____ 05624-3 **THE CHADBOURNE LUCK** #3
Lucia Curzon

_____ 05777-0 **OUT OF A DREAM** #4 Jennifer Rose

_____ 05878-5 **GLITTER GIRL** #5 Jocelyn Day

_____ 05863-7 **AN ARTFUL LADY** #6 Sabina Clark

_____ 05694-4 **EMERALD BAY** #7 Winter Ames

_____ 05776-2 **RAPTURE REGAINED** #8
Serena Alexander

_____ 05801-7 **THE CAUTIOUS HEART** #9
Philippa Heywood

_____ 05907-2 **ALOHA YESTERDAY** #10
Meredith Kingston

All of the above titles are $1.75 per copy

Second Chance at Love ™

All of the above titles are $1.75 per copy

Available at your local bookstore or return this form to:

SECOND CHANCE AT LOVE
The Berkley/Jove Publishing Group
200 Madison Avenue, New York, New York 10016

☐ I've enclosed my completed questionnaire— Publisher will pay the postage.

☐ No questionnaire included. I've enclosed 50¢ for one book, 25¢ each add'l book ($1.25 max). No cash, COD's or stamps. Total amount enclosed:
$_____ in check or money order.

NAME _____

ADDRESS _____

CITY_____ STATE/ZIP_____

Allow six weeks for delivery.   **SK-39**